Richard Cumberland

The West Indian

A Comedy as it is Performed at the Theatre Royal in Drury-Lane

Richard Cumberland

The West Indian
A Comedy as it is Performed at the Theatre Royal in Drury-Lane

ISBN/EAN: 9783744793421

Printed in Europe, USA, Canada, Australia, Japan

Cover: Foto ©Andreas Hilbeck / pixelio.de

More available books at **www.hansebooks.com**

THE

WEST INDIAN:

A

COMEDY.

As it is Performed at the

THEATRE ROYAL

IN

DRURY-LANE

(Quis novus hic Hospes?)

A NEW EDITION.

G. Romney del.   H. Taylor Sc.

LONDON:

Printed for W. GRIFFIN, at GARRICK'S HEAD,
in Catherine Street Strand.
MDCCLXXI.

PROLOGUE.

SPOKEN BY

Mr. REDDISH.

CRITICS, hark forward! noble game and new;
 A fine Weſt Indian ſtarted full in view:
Hot as the ſoil, the clime, which gave him birth,
You'll run him on a burning ſcent to earth;
Yet don't devour him in his hiding place;
Bag him, he'll ſerve you for another chace;
For ſure that country has no feeble claim,
Which ſwells your commerce, and ſupports your fame.
And in this humble ſketch, we hope you'll find,
Some emanations of a noble mind;
Some little touches, which, tho' void of art,
May find perhaps their way into the heart.
Another hero your excuſe implores,
Sent by your ſiſter kingdom to your ſhores;
Doom'd by Religion's too ſevere command,
To fight for bread againſt his native land:
A brave, unthinking, animated rogue,
With here and there a touch upon the brogue;
Laugh, but deſpiſe him not, for on his lip
His errors lie; his heart can never trip.
Others there are——but may we not prevail
To let the gentry tell their own plain tale?
Shall they come in? They'll pleaſe you, if they can;
If not, condemn the bard——but ſpare the *Man.*
For ſpeak, think, act, or write in angry times,
A wiſh to pleaſe is made the worſt of crimes;
Dire ſlander now with black envenom'd dart,
Stands ever arm'd to ſtab you to the heart.

Rouſe,

PROLOGUE.

Rouſe, Britons, rouſe, for honour of your iſle,
Your old good humour; and be ſeen to ſmile.
You ſay we write not like our fathers——true,
Nor were our fathers half ſo ſtrict as you,
Damn'd not each error of the poet's pen,
But judging man, remember'd they were men.
Aw'd into ſilence by the times abuſe,
Sleeps many a wiſe, and many a witty muſe;
We that for mere experiment come out,
Are but the light arm'd rangers on the ſcout:
High on Parnaſſus' lofty ſummit ſtands
The immortal camp; there lie the choſen bands!
But give fair quarter to us puny elves,
The giants then will ſally forth themſelves;
With wit's ſharp weapons vindicate the age,
And drive ev'n *Arthur's* magic from the *Stage.*

Dramatis Personæ.

M E N.

Stockwell, - - - -	Mr. Aickin.
Belcour, - - -	Mr. King.
Captain Dudley, - - -	Mr. Packer.
Charles Dudley, - - -	Mr. Cautherly.
Major O'Flaherty, - -	Mr. Moody.
Stukely, - - -	Mr. J. Aickin.
Fulmer, - - -	Mr. Baddely.
Varland, - - - -	Mr. Parsons.
Servant to Stockwell, - -	Mr. Wheeler.

W O M E N.

Lady Rusport, - -	Mrs. Hopkins.
Charlotte Rusport, - -	Mrs. Abington.
Louisa, daughter to Dudley, -	Mrs. Baddely.
Mrs. Fulmer, - -	Mrs. Egerton.
Lucy, - - - -	Mrs. Love.
Housekeeper belonging to Stockwell, -	Mrs. Bradshaw.

Clerks belonging to Stockwell, servants, sailors, negroes, &c.

SCENE LONDON.

THE

WEST INDIAN.

ACT I. SCENE I.

A MERCHANT's COMPTING HOUSE.

*In an inner room, set off by glass doors, are discovered several
clerks, employed at their desks. A writing table in the
front room.* STOCKWELL *is discovered reading a letter ;*
STUKELY *comes gently out of the back room, and observes
him some time before he speaks.*

Stukely. HE seems disordered : something in that letter ; and I'm afraid of an unpleasant sort.
He has many ventures of great account at sea ; a ship
richly freighted for Barcelona ; another for Lisbon ; and
others expected from Cadiz of still greater value. Besides
these, I know he has many deep concerns in foreign bot-
toms, and underwritings to a vast amount. I'll accost him.
Sir ! Mr. Stockwell !

Stock. Stukely !—Well, have you ship'd the cloths ?

Stukely. I have, Sir ; here's the bill of lading, and copy
of the invoice : the assortments are all compared : Mr.
Traffick will give you the policy upon 'Change.

Stock. 'Tis very well ; lay these papers by ; and no
more of business for a while. Shut the door Stukely ; I
have had long proof of your friendship and fidelity to me ;
a matter of most intimate concern lies on my mind, and
'twill be a sensible relief to unbosom myself to you ; I
have just now been informed of the arrival of the young
West Indian, I have so long been expecting ; you know
who I mean.

B   *Stukely.*

Stukely. Yes, Sir; Mr. Belcour, the young gentleman, who inherited old Belcour's great eftates in Jamaica.

Stock. Hufh, not fo loud; come a little nearer this way. This Belcour is now in London; part of his baggage is already arrived; and I expect him every minute. Is it to be wonder'd at, if his coming throws me into fome agitation, when I tell you, Stukely, he is my fon?

Stukely. Your fon!

Stock. Yes, Sir, my only fon; early in life I accompanied his grandfather to Jamaica as his clerk; he had an only daughter, fomewhat older than myfelf; the mother of this gentleman: it was my chance (call it good or ill) to engage her affections: and, as the inferiority of my condition made it hopelefs to expect her father's confent, her fondnefs provided an expedient, and we were privately married; the iffue of that concealed engagement is, as I have told you, this Belcour.

Stukely. That event, furely, difcovered your connexion.

Stock. You fhall hear. Not many days after our marriage old Belcour fet out for England; and, during his abode here, my wife was, with great fecrefy, delivered of this fon. Fruitful in expedients to difguife her fituation, without parting from her infant, fhe contrived to have it laid and received at her door as a foundling. After fome time her father returned, having left me here; in one of thofe favourable moments, that decide the fortunes of profperous men, this child was introduced; from that inftant, he treated him as his own, gave him his name, and brought him up in his family.

Stukely. And did you never reveal this fecret, either to old Belcour, or your fon?

Stock. Never.

Stukely. Therein you furprize me; a merchant of your eminence, and a member of the Britifh parliament, might furely afpire, without offence, to the daughter of a planter. In this cafe too, natural affection would prompt to a difcovery.

Stock. Your remark is obvious; nor could I have perfifted in this painful filence, but in obedience to the dying injunctions of a beloved wife. The letter, you found me reading, conveyed thofe injunctions to me; it was dictated in her laft illnefs, and almoft in the article of death; (you'll fpare me the recital of it) fhe there conjures me, in terms

28

as folemn, as they are affecting, never to reveal the fecret of our marriage, or withdraw my fon, while her father furviv'd.

Stukely. But on what motives did your unhappy lady found thefe injunctions?

Stock. Principally, I believe, from apprehenfion on my account, left old Belcour, on whom at her deceafe I wholly depended, fhould withdraw his protection: in part from confideration of his repofe, as well knowing the difcovery would deeply affect his fpirit, which was haughty, vehement, and unforgiving: and laftly, in regard to the intereft of her infant, whom he had warmly adopted; and for whom, in cafe of a difcovery, every thing was to be dreaded from his refentment. And, indeed, though the alteration in my condition might have juftified me in difcovering myfelf, yet I always thought my fon fafer in trufting to the caprice than to the juftice of his grand-father. My judgment has not fuffered by the event; old Belcour is dead, and has bequeathed his whole eftate to him we are fpeaking of.

Stukely. Now then you are no longer bound to fecrefy.

Stock. True: but before I publickly reveal myfelf, I could wifh to make fome experiment of my fon's difpofition: this can only be done by letting his fpirit take its courfe without reftraint; by thefe means, I think I fhall difcover much more of his real character under the title of his merchant, than I fhould under that of his father.

S C E N E II.

A Sailor enters, ufhering in feveral black Servants, carrying portmanteaus, trunks, &c.

Sailor. Save your honour! is your name Stockwell, pray?

Stock. It is.

Sailor. Part of my mafter Belcour's baggage an't pleafe you; there's another cargo not far a-ftern of us; and the cock-fwain has got charge of the dumb creatures.

Stock. Pr'ythee, friend, what dumb creatures do you fpeak of; has Mr. Belcour brought over a collection of wild beafts?

Sailor. No, Lord love him; no, not he: let me fee; there's two green monkies, a pair of grey parrots, a Jamaica fow and pigs, and a Mangrove dog; that's all.

Stock. Is that all ?

Sailor. Yes, your honour; yes, that's all; blefs his heart a'might have brought over the whole ifland if he would ; a didn't leave a dry eye in it.

Stock. Indeed ! Stukely, fhew 'em where to beftow their baggage. Follow that gentleman.

Sailor. Come, bear a hand, my lads, bear a hand.

[*Exit with* Stukely *and Servants.*

Stock. If the principal tallies with his purveyors, he muft be a fingular fpectacle in this place : he has a friend, however, in this fea-faring fellow ; 'tis no bad prognoftic of a man's heart, when his fhip-mates gives him a good word. [*Exit.*

S C E N E III.

Scene changes to a drawing room, a Servant difcovered fetting the chairs by, &c. *a Woman Servant enters to him.*

Houfek. Why, what a fufs does our good mafter put himfelf in about this Weft Indian : fee what a bill of fare I've been forced to draw out : feven and nine I'll affure you, and only a family dinner as he calls it : why if my Lord Mayor was expected, there couldn't be a greater to-do about him.

Servant. I wifh to my heart you had but feen the loads of trunks, boxes, and portmanteaus he has fent hither. An ambaffador's baggage, with all the fmuggled goods of his family, does not exceed it.

Houfek. A fine pickle he'll put the houfe into : had he been mafter's own fon, and a Chriftian Englifhman, there cou'd not be more rout than there is about this Creolian, as they call 'em.

Servant. No matter for that ; he's very rich, and that's fufficient. They fay he has rum and fugar enough belonging to him, to make all the water in the Thames into punch. But I fee my mafter's coming. [*Exeunt.*

S C E N E IV.

STOCKWELL *enters, followed by a Servant.*

Stock. Where is Mr. Belcour ? Who brought this note from him ?

Servant.

Servant. A waiter from the London Tavern, Sir; he says the young gentleman is juft dreft, and will be with you directly.

Stock. Shew him in when he arrives.

Servant. I fhall, Sir. I'll have a peep at him firft, however; I've a great mind to fee this outlandifh fpark. The failor fellow fays he'll make rare doings amongft us.
(afide.)

Stock. You need not wait; leave me.   [*Exit Servant.* Let me fee (*reads.*)

" Sir,

" I write to you under the hands of the hair-dreffer; " as foon as I have made myfelf decent, and flipped on " fome frefh cloaths, I will have the honour of paying " you my devoirs.

" Yours,

" Belcour."

He write's at his eafe; for he's unconfcious to whom his letter is addreffed; but what a palpitation does it throw my heart into; a father's heart! 'Tis an affecting interview; when my eyes meet a fon, whom yet they never faw, where fhall I find conftancy to fupport it? Should he refemble his mother, I am overthrown. All the letters I have had from him, (for I induftrioufly drew him into a correfpondence with me) befpeak him of quick and ready underftanding. All the reports I ever received, give me favourable impreffions of his character, wild, perhaps, as the manner of his country is, but, I truft, not frantic or unprincipled.

S C E N E   V.

SERVANT *enters.*

Servant. Sir, the foreign gentleman is come.

Another SERVANT.

Servant. Mr. Belcour.

BELCOUR *enters.*

Stock. Mr Belcour, I'm rejoiced to fee you; you're welcome to Engand.

Bel. I thank you heartily, good Mr. Stockwell; you and I have long converfed at a diftance; now we
are

are met; and the pleasure this meeting gives me, amply compensates for the perils I have run through in accomplishing it.

Stock. What perils, Mr. Belcour? I could not have thought you would have made a bad passage at this time o'year.

Bel. Nor did we: courier like, we came posting to your shores, upon the pinions of the swiftest gales that ever blew; 'tis upon English ground all my difficulties have arisen; 'tis the passage from the river-side I complain of.

Stock. Ay, indeed! What obstructions can you have met between this and the river-side?

Bel. Innumerable! Your town's as full of defiles as the Island of Corsica; and, I believe, they are as obstinately defended: so much hurry, bustle, and confusion, on your quays; so many sugar-casks, porter-butts, and common council-men, in your streets, that, unless a man marched with artillery in his front, 'tis more than the labour of a Hercules can effect, to make any tolerable way through your town.

Stock. I am sorry you have been so incommoded.

Bel. Why, faith, 'twas all my own fault: accustomed to a land of slaves, and out of patience with the whole tribe of custom-house extortioners, boat-men, tidewaiters, and water-bailiffs, that beset me on all sides, worse than a swarm of musquetoes, I proceeded a little too roughly to brush them away with my rattan; the sturdy rogues took this in dudgeon, and beginning to rebel, the mob chose different sides, and a furious scuffle ensued; in the course of which, my person and apparel suffered so much, that I was obliged to step into the first tavern to refit, before I could make my approaches in any decent trim.

Stock. All without is as I wish; dear Nature add the rest, and I am happy (*aside.*) Well, Mr. Belcour, 'tis a rough sample you have had of my countrymen's spirit; but, I trust, you'll not think the worse of them for it.

Bel. Not at all, not at all; I like 'em the better; was I only a visitor, I might, perhaps, wish them a little more tractable; but, as a fellow subject, and a sharer in their freedom, I applaud their spirit, though I feel the effects of it in every bone of my skin.

Stock.

Stock. That's well; I like that well. How gladly I could fall upon his neck, and own myself his father! *(aside.)*

Bel. Well, Mr. Stockwell, for the first time in my life, here am I in England; at the fountain-head of pleasure, in the land of beauty, of arts, and elegancies. My happy stars have given me a good estate, and the conspiring winds have blown me hither to spend it.

Stock. To use it, not to waste it, I should hope; to treat it, Mr. Belcour, not as a vassal, over whom you have a wanton and a despotic power; but as a subject, which you are bound to govern with a temperate and restrained authority.

Bel. True, Sir; most truly said; mine's a commission, not a right: I am the offspring of distress, and every child of sorrow is my brother; while I have hands to hold, therefore, I will hold them open to mankind: but, Sir, my passions are my masters; they take me where they will; and oftentimes they leave to reason and to virtue nothing but my wishes and my sighs.

Stock. Come, come, the man who can accuse corrects himself.

Bel. Ah! that's an office I am weary of: I wish a friend would take it up: I would to Heaven you had leisure for the employ; but, did you drive a trade to the four corners of the world, you would not find the task so toilsome as to keep me free from faults.

Stock. Well, I am not discouraged: this candour tells me I should not have the fault of self-conceit to combat; that, at least, is not amongst the number.

Bel. No; if I knew that man on earth who thought more humbly of me than I do of myself, I would take up his opinion, and forego my own.

Stock. And, was I to chuse a pupil, it should be one of your complexion: so if you'll come along with me, we'll agree upon your admission, and enter on a course of lectures directly.

Bel. With all my heart.   [*Exeunt.*

S C E N E   VI.

Scene changes to a room in LADY RUSPORT's *house.*

LADY RUSPORT *and* CHARLOTTE.

L. Rus. Miss Rusport, I desire to hear no more of Captain Dudley and his destitute family: not a shilling of mine fhall ever crofs the hands of any of them: becaufe my fifter chofe to marry a beggar, am I bound to fupport him and his pofterity?

Char. I think you are.

L. Ruf. You think I am; and pray where do you find the law that tells you fo?

Char. I am not proficient enough to quote chapter and verfe; but I take charity to be a main claufe in the great ftatute of chriftianity.

L. Ruf. I fay charity, indeed! And pray, Mifs, are you fure that it is charity, pure charity, which moves you to plead for Captain Dudley? Amongft all your pity, do you find no fpice of a certain anti-fpiritual paffion, called love? Don't miftake yourfelf; you are no faint, child, believe me; and, I am apt to think, the diftreffes of old Dudley, and of his daughter into the bargain, would never break your heart, if there was not a certain young fellow of two and twenty in the cafe; who, by the happy recommendation of a good perfon, and the brilliant appointments of an enfigncy, will, if I am not miftaken, cozen you out of a fortune of twice twenty thoufand pounds, as foon as ever you are of age to beftow it upon him.

Char. A nephew of your ladyfhip's can never want any other recommendation with me; and, if my partiality for Charles Dudley is acquitted by the reft of the world, I hope Lady Rufport will not condemn me for it.

L. Ruf. I condemn you! I thank Heaven, Mifs Rufport, I am no ways refponfible for your conduct; nor is it any concern of mine how you difpofe of yourfelf; you are not my daughter; and, when I married your father, poor Sir Stephen Rufport, I found you a forward fpoiled Mifs of fourteen, far above being inftructed me.

Char. Perhaps your ladyfhip calls this inftruction.

L. Ruf. You're ftrangely pert; but 'tis no wonder: your mother, I'm told was a fine lady; and according to the modern ftile of education you was brought up. It was not fo in my young days; there was then fome decorum in the world, fome fubordination, as the great Locke expreffes it. Oh! 'twas an edifying fight, to fee the regular deportment obferved in our family: no gigling, no goffiping was going on there; my good father, Sir Oliver Roundhead, never was feen to laugh himfelf, nor ever allowed it in his children.

Char.

Char. Ay; thofe were happy times, indeed.

L. Ruf. But, in this forward age, we have coquets in the egg-fhell, and philofophers in the cradle; girls of fifteen that lead the fafhion in new caps and new opinions, that have their fentiments and their fenfations; and the idle fops encourage 'em in it: O' my confcience, I wonder what it is the men can fee in fuch babies.

Char. True, madam; but all men do not overlook the maturer beauties of your ladyfhip's age, witnefs your admirer Major Dennis O'Flaherty; there's an example of fome difcernment; I declare to you, when your ladyfhip is by, the Major takes no more notice of me than if I was part of the furniture of your chamber.

L. Ruf. The Major, child, has travelled through various kingdoms and climates, and has more enlarged notions of female merit than falls to the lot of an Englifh home-bred lover; in moft other countries, no woman on your fide forty would ever be named in a polite circle.

Char. Right, Madam; I've been told that in Vienna they have coquets upon crutches, and Venufes in their grand climacteric; a lover there celebrates the wrinkles, not the dimples, in his miftrefs's face. The Major, I think, has ferved in the imperial army.

L. Ruf. Are you piqu'd, my young madam? Had my fifter, Louifa, yielded to the addreffes of one of Major O'Flaherty's perfon and appearance, fhe would have had fome excufe: but to run away, as fhe did, at the age of fixteen too, with a man of old Dudley's fort——

Char. Was, in my opinion, the moft venial trefpafs that ever girl of fixteen committed; of a noble family, an engaging perfon, ftrict honour, and found underftanding; what accomplifhment was there wanting in Captain Dudley, but that which the prodigality of his anceftors had deprived him of?

L. Ruf. They left him as much as he deferves; hasn't the old man captain's half pay? And is not the fon an enfign?

Char. An enfign! Alas, poor Charles! Would to Heaven he knew what my heart feels and fuffers for his fake.

SERVANT enters.

Ser. Enfign Dudley to wait upon your ladyfhip.

C *L. Ruf.*

L. Ruf. Who! Dudley! What can have brought him to town?

Char. Dear madam, 'tis Charles Dudley, 'tis your nephew.

L. Ruf. Nephew! I renounce him as my nephew; Sir Oliver renounced him as his grandfon: wasn't he fon of the eldeft daughter, and only ma:e defcendant of Sir Oliver; and didn't he cut him off with a fhilling? Didn't the poor dear good man leave his whole fortune to me, except a fmall annuity to my maiden fifter, who fpoiled her conftitution with nurfing him? And, depend upon it, not a penny of that fortune fhall ever be difpofed of otherwife than according to the will of the donor. (CHARLES DUDLEY *enters.*) So young man, whence come you? What brings you to town?

Charles. If there is any offence in my coming to town, your ladyfhip is in fome degree refponfible for it, for part of my errand was to pay my duty here.

L. Ruf. I hope you have fome better excufe than all this.

Charles. 'Tis true, madam, I have other motives; but, if I confider my trouble repaid by the pleafure I now enjoy, I fhould hope my aunt would not think my company the lefs welcome for the value I fet upon her's.

L. Ruf. Coxcomb! And where is your father, child; and your fifter? Are they in town too?

Charles. They are.

L. Ruf. Ridiculous! I don't know what people do in London, who have no money to fpend in it.

Char. Dear madam, fpeak more kindly to your nephew; how can you opprefs a youth of his fenfibility?

L. Ruf. Mifs Rufport, I infift upon your retiring to your apartment; when I want your advice I'll fend to you. (*Exit* CHARLOTTE.) So you have put on a red coat too, as well as your father; 'tis plain what value you fet upon the good advice Sir Oliver ufed to give you; how often has he caution'd you againft the army?

Charles. Had it pleafed my grandfather to enable me to have obeyed his caution, I would have done it; but you well know how deftitute I am; and 'tis not to be wonder'd at if I prefer the fervice of my king to that of any other mafter.

L. Ruf. Well, well, take your own courfe; 'tis no concern of mine: you never confulted me.

Charles.

Charles. I frequently wrote to your ladyship, but could obtain no answer; and, since my grandfather's death, this is the first opportunity I have had of waiting upon you.

L. Ruf. I must desire you not to mention the death of that dear good man in my hearing, my spirits cannot support it.

Charles. I shall obey you: permit me to say, that, as that event has richly supplied you with the materials of bounty, the distresses of my family can furnish you with objects of it.

L. Ruf. The distresses of your family, child, are quite out of the question at present; had Sir Oliver been pleased to consider them, I should have been well content; but he has absolutely taken no notice of you in his will, and that to me must and shall be a law. Tell your father and your sister I totally disapprove of their coming up to town.

Charles. Must I tell my father that before your ladyship knows the motive that brought him hither? Allur'd by the offer of exchanging for a commission on full pay, the veteran, after thirty years service, prepares to encounter the fatal heats of Senegambia; but wants a small supply to equip him for the expedition.

SERVANT *enters.*

Ser. Major O'Flaherty to wait on your ladyship.

MAJOR *enters.*

O'Fla. Spare your speeches, young man; don't you think her ladyship can take my word for that? I hope, madam, 'tis evidence enough of my being present, when I've the honour of telling you so myself.

L Ruf. Major O'Flaherty, I am rejoiced to see you. Nephew Dudley, you perceive I'm engaged.

Charles. I shall not intrude upon your ladyship's more agreeable engagements. I presume I have my answer.

L. Ruf. Your answer, child! What answer can you possibly expect; or how can your romantic father suppose that I am to abet him in all his idle and extravagant undertakings? Come, Major, let me shew you the way into my dressing-room; and let us leave this young adventurer to his meditation. [*Exit.*

O'Fla. I follow you, my lady. Young gentleman, your obedient! Upon my conscience, as fine a young fellow as I wou'd wish to clap my eyes on: he might have an-

C 2   swer'd

fwer'd my falute, however—well, let it pafs ; Fortune, perhaps, frowns upon the poor lad ; fhe's a damn'd flippery lady, and very apt to jilt us poor fellows, that wear cockades in our hats. Fare-thee-well, honey, whoever thou art.   [*Exit.*

Charles. So much for the virtues of a puritan ; out upon it, her heart is flint ; yet that woman, that aunt of mine, without one worthy particle in her compofition, wou'd, I dare be fworn, as foon fet her foot in a peft-houfe, as in a play-houfe.   [*going.*

(Miss Rusport *enters to him.*)

Char. Stop, ftay a little, Charles, whither are you going in fuch hafte ?

Charles. Madam ; Mifs Rufport ; what are your commands ?

Char. Why fo referved ? We had ufed to anfwer to no other names than thofe of Charles and Charlotte.

Charles. What ails you ? you've been weeping.

Char. No, no ; or if I have—your eyes are full too ; but I have a thoufand things to fay to you : before you go, tell me, I conjure you, where you are to be found ; here, give me your direction ; write it upon the back of this vifiting-ticket—Have you a pencil ?

Charles. I have : but why fhou'd you defire to find us out ? 'tis a poor little inconvenient place ; my fifter has no apartment fit to receive you in.

SERVANT *enters.*

Ser. Madam, my lady defires your company directly.

Char. I am coming—well, have you wrote it ? Give it me. O Charles ! either you do not, or you will not underftand me.   (*Exeunt feverally.*)

END OF THE FIRST ACT.

ACT II. SCENE I.

A Room in FULMER's *House.*

FULMER *and* MRS. FULMER.

Mrs. Ful. WHY, how you sit, musing and mopeing, sighing and desponding! I'm ashamed of you, Mr. Fulmer: is this the country you described to me, a second Eldorado, rivers of gold and rocks of diamonds? You found me in a pretty snug retir'd way of life at Bologne, out of the noise and bustle of the world, and wholly at my ease ; you, indeed, was upon the wing, with a fiery persecution at your back : but, like a true son of *Loyola*, you had then a thousand ingenious devices to repair your fortune; and this, your native country was to be the scene of your performances: fool that I was, to be inveigled into it by you : but, thank Heaven, our partnership is revocable ; I am not your wedded wife, praised be my stars! for what have we got, whom have we gull'd but ourselves ; which of all your trains has taken fire; even this poor expedient of your bookseller's shop seems abandoned ; for if a chance customer drops in, who is there, pray, to help him to what he wants ?

Ful. Patty, you know it is not upon slight grounds that I despair ; there had us'd to be a livelihood to be pick'd up in this country, both for the honest and dishonest : I have tried each walk, and am likely to starve at last: there is not a point to which the wit and faculty of man can turn, that I have not set mine to; but in vain, I am beat through every quarter of the compass.

Mrs. Ful. Ah ! common efforts all : strike me a masterstroke, Mr. Fulmer, if you wish to make any figure in this country.

Ful. But where, how, and what ? I have bluster'd for prerogative; I have bellowed for freedom ; I have offer'd to serve my country; I have engaged to betray it ; a master-stroke, truly ; why, I have talked treason, writ treason, and if a man can't live by that he can live by nothing. Here I set up as a bookseller, why men left off reading; and if I was to turn butcher, I believe, o'my conscience they'd leave off eating.

CAPT.

(CAPT. DUDLEY *croffes the ftage.*)

Mrs. Ful. Why there now's your lodger, old Captain Dudley, as he calls himfelf; there's no flint without fire; fomething might be ftruck out of him, if you'd the wit to find the way.

Ful. Hang him, an old dry fkin'd curmudgeon; you may as well think to get truth out of a court'er, or candour out of a critic: I can make nothing of him; befides, he's poor, and therefore not for our purpofe.

Mrs. Ful. The mere fool he! Wou'd any man be poor that had fuch a prodigy in his poffeffion?

Ful. His daughter, you mean; fhe is, indeed, uncommonly beautiful.

Mrs. Ful. Beautiful! Why fhe need only be feen, to have the firft men in the kingdom at her feet. Egad, I wifh I had the leafing of her beauty; what would fome of our young Nabobs give——?

Ful. Hufh! here comes the captain; good girl, leave us to ourfelves, and let me try what I can make of him.

Mrs. Ful. Captain, truly! i'faith I'd have a regiment, had I fuch a daughter, before I was three months older.

[*Exit.*

S C E N E   III.

CAPTAIN DUDLEY *enters to him.*

Ful. Captain Dudley, good morning to you.

Dud. Mr. Fulmer, I have borrowed a book from your fhop; 'tis the fixth volume of my deceafed friend Triftram: he is a flattering writer to us poor foldiers; and the divine ftory of Le Fevre, which makes part of this book, in my opinion of it, does honour not to its author only, but to human nature.

Ful. He's an author I keep in the way of trade, but one I never relifh'd: he is much too loofe and profligate for my tafte.

Dud. That's being too fevere: I hold him to be a moralift in the nobleft fenfe; he plays indeed with the fancy, and fometimes perhaps too wantonly; but while he thus defignedly mafks his main attack, he comes at once upon the heart; refines, amends it, foftens it; beats down each felfifh barrier from about it, and opens every fluice of pity and benevolence.

Ful. We of the catholic perfuafion are not much bound

to

to him.——Well, Sir, I ſhall not oppoſe your opinion ; a favourite author is like a favourite miſtreſs ; and there you know, Captain, no man likes to have his taſte arraigned.

Dud. Upon my word, Sir, I don't know what a man likes in that caſe ; 'tis an experiment I never made.

Ful. Sir!—Are you ſerious ?

Dud. 'Tis of little conſequence whether you think ſo.

Ful. What a formal old prig it is ! (*aſide.*) I apprehend you, Sir ; you ſpeak with caution ; you are married ?

Dud. I have been.

Ful. And this young lady, which accompanies you—

Dud. Paſſes for my daughter.

Ful. Paſſes for his daughter ! humph—(*aſide.*) She is exceedingly beautiful, finely accompliſhed, of a moſt enchanting ſhape and air.

Dud. You are much too partial ; ſhe has the greateſt defect a woman can have.

Ful. How ſo, pray ?

Dud. She has no fortune.

Ful. Rather ſay that you have none ; and that's a ſore defect in one of your years, Captain Dudley : you've ſerved, no doubt ?

Dud. Familiar Coxcomb ! But I'll humour him (*aſide.*)

Ful. A cloſe old fox ! But I'll unkennel him (*aſide.*)

Dud. Above thirty years I've been in the ſervice, Mr. Fulmer.

Ful. I gueſs'd as much ; I laid it at no leſs : why 'tis a weariſome time ; 'tis an apprenticeſhip to a profeſſion, fit only for a patriarch. But preferment muſt be cloſely followed : you never could have been ſo far behind hand in the chace, unleſs you had palpably miſtaken your way. You'll pardon me, but I begin to perceive you have lived in the world, not with it.

Dud. It may be ſo ; and you, perhaps, can give me better council. I'm now ſoliciting a favour ; an exchange to a company on full pay ; nothing more ; and yet I meet a thouſand bars to that ; tho', without boaſting, I ſhould think the certificate of ſervices, which I ſent in, might have purchaſed that indulgence to me.

Ful. Who thinks or cares about 'em ? Certificate of ſervices, indeed ! Send in a certificate of your fair daughter ; carry her in your hand with you.

Dud.

Dud. What! Who! My daughter! Carry my daughter! Well, and what then?

Ful. Why, then your fortune's made, that's all.

Dud. I underſtand you : and this you call knowledge of the world? Deſpicable knowledge; but, ſirrah, I will have you know—*(threatening him.)*

Ful. Help! Who's within? Wou'd you ſtrike me, Sir; wou'd you lift up your hand againſt a man in his own houſe?

Dud. In a church, if he dare inſult the poverty of a man of honour.

Ful. Have a care what you do ; remember there is ſuch a thing in law as an aſſault and battery ; ay, and ſuch trifling forms as warrants and indictments.

Dud. Go, Sir; you are too mean for my reſentment: 'tis that, and not the law, protects you.   Hence!

Ful. An old, abſurd, incorrigible blockhead! I'll be reveng'd of him *(aſide.)*

S C E N E   III.

Y O U N G   D U D L E Y *enters to him.*

Charles. What is the matter, Sir? Sure I heard an out-cry as I enter'd the houſe.

Dud. Not unlikely; our landlord and his wife are for ever wrangling.—Did you find your aunt Dudley at home?

Charles. I did.

Dud. And what was your reception?

Charles. Cold as our poverty and her pride could make it.

Dud. You told her the preſſing occaſion I had for a ſmall ſupply to equip me for this exchange ; has ſhe granted me the relief I aſked?

Charles. Alas! Sir, ſhe has peremptorily refuſed it.

Dud. That's hard; that's hard, indeed! My petition was for a ſmall ſum; ſhe has refuſed it, you ſay: well, be it ſo ; I muſt not complain.   Did you ſee the broker about the inſurance on my life?

Charles. There again I am the meſſenger of ill news ; I can raiſe no money, ſo fatal is the climate: alas! that ever my father ſhould be ſent to periſh in ſuch a place!

S C E N E   IV.

MISS D U D L E Y *enters haſtily.*

Dud. Louiſa, what's the matter? you ſeem frighted.

Lou. I am, indeed: coming from Mifs Rufport's, I met a young gentleman in the ftreets, who has befet me in the ftrangeft manner.

Charles. Infufferable! Was he rude to you?

Lou. I cannot fay he was abfolutely rude to me, but he was very importunate to fpeak to me, and once or twice attempted to lift up my hat: he follow'd me to the corner of the ftreet, and there I gave him the flip.

Dud. You muft walk no more in the ftreets, child, without me, or your brother.

Lou. O Charles! Mifs Rufport defires to fee you directly; Lady Rufport is gone out, and fhe has fomething particular to fay to you.

Charles. Have you any commands for me, Sir?

Dud. None, my dear; by all means wait upon Mifs Rufport. Come, Louifa, I fhall defire you to go up to your chamber, and compofe yourfelf.   [*Exeunt.*

S C E N E V.

BELCOUR *enters, after peeping in at the door.*

Bel. Not a foul, as I'm alive. Why, what an odd fort of a houfe is this! Confound the little jilt, fhe has fairly given me the flip. A plague upon this London, I fhall have no luck in it: fuch a crowd, and fuch a hurry, and fuch a number of fhops, and one fo like the other, that whether the wench turn'd into this houfe or the next, or whether fhe went up ftairs or down ftairs, (for there's a world above and a world below, it feems) I declare, I know no more than if I was in the Blue Mountains. In the name of all the devils at once, why did fhe run away? If every handfome girl I meet in this town is to lead me fuch a wild-goofe chace, I had better have ftay'd in the torrid zone: I fhall be wafted to the fize of a fugar-cane: what fhall I do? give the chace up? hang it, that's cowardly: fhall I, a true-born fon of Phœbus, fuffer this little nimble-footed Daphne to efcape me?——" Forbid it honour, and forbid it love." Hufh! hufh! here fhe comes! Oh! the devil! What tawdry thing have we got here?

MRS. FULMER *enters to him.*

Mrs. Ful. Your humble fervant, Sir.

Bel. Your humble fervant, Madam.

D

Mrs. Ful.

Mrs. Ful. A fine fummer's day, Sir.

Bel. Yes, Ma'am, and fo cool, that if the calendar didn't call it July, I fhou'd fwear it was January.

Mrs. Ful. Sir!.

Bel. Madam!

Mrs. Ful. Do you wifh to fpeak to Mr. Fulmer, Sir?

Bel. Mr. Fulmer, Madam? I havn't the honour of knowing fuch a perfon.

Mis. Ful. No, I'll be fworn, have you not; thou art much too pretty a fellow, and too much of a gentleman, to be an author thyfelf, or to have any thing to fay to thofe that are fo. 'Tis the Captain, I fuppofe, you are waiting for.

Bel. I rather fufpect it is the Captain's wife.

Mrs. Ful. The Captain has no wife, Sir.

Bel. No wife! I'm heartily forry for it; for then fhe's his miftrefs; and that I take to be the more defperate cafe of the two: pray, Madam, wasn't there a lady juft now turn'd into your houfe? 'Twas with her I wifh'd to fpeak.

Mrs. Ful. What fort of a lady, pray?

Bel. One of the lovelieft fort my eyes ever beheld; young, tall, frefh, fair; in fhort, a goddefs.

Mrs. Ful. Nay, but dear, dear Sir, now I'm fure you flatter; for 'twas me you followed into the fhop-door this minute,

Bel. You! No, no, take my word for it, it was not you, Madam.

Mrs. Ful. But what is it you laugh at?

Bel. Upon my foul, I afk your pardon; but it was not you, believe me; be affur'd it wasn't.

Mrs. Ful. Well, Sir, I fhall not contend for the honour of being notic'd by you; I hope you think you woudn't have been the firft man that notic'd me in the ftreets; however, this i'm pofitive of, that no living woman but myfelf has enter'd thefe doors this morning.

Bel. Why then I'm miftaken in the houfe, that's all; for 'tis not humanly poffible I can be fo far out in the lady *(going)*

Mrs. Ful. Coxcomb! But hold—a thought occurs; as fure as can be he has feen Mifs Dudley. A word with you, young gentleman; come back.

Bel. Well, what's your pleafure?

Mrs. Ful. You feem greatly captivated with this young lady; are you apt to fall in love thus at firft fight?

Bel. Oh, yes: 'tis the only way I can ever fall in love; any man may tumble into a pit by furprize, none but a fool would walk into one by choice.

Mrs. Ful. You are a hafty lover it feems; have you fpirit to be a generous one? They that will pleafe the eye muftn't fpare the purfe.

Bel. Try me; put me to the proof; bring me to an interview with the dear girl that has thus captivated me, and fee whether I have fpirit to be grateful.

Mrs. Ful. But how, pray, am I to know the girl you have fet your heart on?

Bel. By an undeferibable grace, that accompanies every look and action that falls from her: there can be but one fuch woman in the world, and nobody can miftake that one.

Mrs. Ful. Well, if I fhould ftumble upon this angel in my walks, where am I to find you? What's your name?

Bel. Upon my foul, I can't tell you my name.

Mrs. Ful. Not tell me! Why fo?

Bel. Becaufe I don't know what it is myfelf; as yet I have no name.

Mrs. Ful. No name!

Bel. None; a friend, indeed, lent me his; but he forbad me to ufe it on any unworthy occafion.

Mrs. Ful. But where is your place of abode?

Bel. I have none; I never flept a night in England in my life.

Mrs Ful. Hey-day!

S C E N E   VI.

F U L M E R *enters.*

Ful. A fine cafe, truly, in a free country; a pretty pafs things are come to, if a man is to be affaulted in his own houfe.

Mrs. Ful. Who has affaulted you, my dear?

Ful. Who! why this Captain Drawcanfir, this old Dudley, my lodger; but I'll unlodge him; I'll unharbour him, I warrant.

Mrs. Ful. Hufh! hufh! Hold your tongue man; pocket the affront, and be quiet; I've a fcheme on foot will pay you a hundred beatings. Why you furprize me, Mr. Fulmer; Captain Dudley affault you! Impoffible.

Ful.

Ful. Nay, I can't call it an abfolute affault; but he threatened me.

Mrs. Ful. Oh, was that all? I thought how it would turn out—A likely thing, truly, for a perfon of his obliging compaffionate turn: no, no, poor Captain Dudley, he has forrows and diftreffes enough of his own to employ his fpirits, without fetting them againft other people. Make it up as faft as you can: watch this gentleman out; follow him wherever he goes; and bring me word who and what he is; be fure you don't lofe fight of him; I've other bufinefs in hand. [*Exit.*

Bel. Pray, Sir, what forrows and diftreffes have befallen this old gentleman you fpeak of?

Ful. Poverty, difappointment, and all the diftreffes attendant thereupon: forrow enough of all confcience: I foon found how it was with him by his way of living, low enough of all reafon; but what I overheard this morning put it out of all doubt.

Bel. What did you overhear this morning?

Ful. Why, it feems he wants to join his regiment, and has been beating the town over to raife a little money for that purpofe upon his pay; but the climate, I find, where he is going, is fo unhealthy, that nobody can be found to lend him any.

Bel. Why then your town is a damn'd good-for-nothing town: and I wifh I had never come into it.

Ful. That's what I fay, Sir; the hard-heartednefs of fome folks is unaccountable. There's an old Lady Rufport, a near relation of this gentleman's; fhe lives hard by here, oppofite to Stockwell's, the great merchant; he fent to her a begging, but to no purpofe; though fhe is as rich as a Jew, fhe would not furnifh him with a farthing.

Bel. Is the Captain at home?

Ful. He is up ftairs, Sir.

Bel. Will you take the trouble to defire him to ftep hither? I want to fpeak to him.

Ful. I'll fend him to you directly. I don't know what to make of this young man; but, if I live, I will find him out, or know the reafon why. [*Exit.*

Bel. I've loft the girl it feems; that's clear: fhe was the firft object of my purfuit; but the cafe of this poor officer touches me; and, after all, there may be as much true delight in refcuing a fellow creature from diftrefs, as there would

would be in plunging one into it——But let me fee; it's a point that muft be managed with fome delicacy—Apropos! there's pen and ink—I've ftruck upon a method that will do (*writes.*) Ay, ay, this is the very thing; 'twas devilifh lucky I happen'd to have thefe bills about me. There, there, fare you well; I'm glad to be rid of you; you ftood a chance of being worfe applied, I can tell you (*enclofes and feals the paper.*)

SCENE VII.

FULMER *brings in* DUDLEY.

Ful. That's the gentleman, Sir. I fhall make bold, however, to lend an ear.

Dud. Have you any commands for me, Sir ?

Bel. Your name is Dudley, Sir—— ?

Dud. It is.

Bel. You command a company, I think, Captain Dudley ?

Dud. I did : I am now upon half-pay.

Bel. You've ferv'd fome time ?

Dud. A pretty many years ; long enough to fee fome people of more merit, and better intereft than myfelf, made general officers.

Bel. Their merit I may have fome doubt of; their intereft I can readily give credit to; there is little promotion to be look'd for, in your profeffion, I believe, without friends, Captain ?

Dud. I believe fo too : have you any other bufinefs with me, may I afk ?

Bel. Your patience for a moment. I was informed you was about to join your regiment in diftant quarters abroad.

Dud. I have been foliciting an exchange to a company on full-pay, quarter'd at James's Fort, in Senegambia; but, I'm afraid, I muft drop the undertaking.

Bel. Why fo, pray ?

Dud. Why fo, Sir ? 'Tis a home-queftion for a perfect ftranger to put ; there is fomething very particular in all this.

Bel. If it is not impertinent, Sir, allow me to afk you what reafon you have for defpairing of fuccefs.

Dud. Why really, Sir, mine is an obvious reafon for a foldier to have—Want of money ; fimply that.

Bel.

Bel. May I beg to know the fum you have occafion for?

Dud. Truly, Sir, I cannot exactly tell you on a fudden; nor is it, I fuppofe, of any great confequence to you
to be informed; but I fhould guefs, in the grofs, that two
hundred pounds would ferve.

Bel. And do you find a difficulty in raifing that fum
upon your pay? 'Tis done every day.

Dud. The nature of the climate makes it difficult: I
can get no one to infure my life.

Bel. Oh! that's a circumftance may make for you, as
well as againft: in fhort, Captain Dudley, it fo happens,
that I can command the fum of two hundred pounds: feek
no farther; I'll accomodate you with it upon eafy terms.

Dud. Sir! do I underftand you rightly?—I beg your
pardon; but am I to believe that you are in earneft?

Bel. What is your furprize? Is it an uncommon thing
for a gentleman to fpeak truth? Or is it incredible that one
fellow creature fhould affift another?

Dud. I afk your pardon—May I beg to know to whom?
Do you propofe this in the way of bufinefs?

Bel. Entirely: I have no other bufinefs on earth.

Dud. Indeed! you are not a broker, I'm perfuaded.

Bel. I am not.

Dud. Nor an army agent I think?

Bel. I hope you will not think the worfe of me for being
neither; in fhort, Sir, if you will perufe this paper, it will
explain to you who I am, and upon what terms I act;
while you read it, I will ftep home, and fetch the money;
and we will conclude the bargain without lofs of time. In
the mean while, good day to you.   [*Exit haftily.*

Dud. Humph! there's fomething very odd in all this—
let me fee what we've got here—This paper is to tell me
who he is, and what are his terms: in the name of wonder, why has he fealed it! Hey-dey! what's here? Two
Bank notes, of a hundred each! I can't comprehend what
this means. Hold; here's a writing; perhaps that will
fhow me. " Accept this trifle; purfue your fortune, and
profper." Am I in a dream? Is this a reality?

SCENE VIII.

Enter MAJOR O'FLAHERTY.

Ma. Save you, my dear! Is it you now that are Captain
Dudley, I would afk?——Whuh! What's the hurry the

man's in? If 'tis the lad that run out of the shop you would overtake, you might as well stay where you are; by my soul he's as nimble as a Croat, you are a full hour's march in his rear—Ay, faith, you may as well turn back, and give over the pursuit; well, Captain Dudley, if that's your name, there's a letter for you. Read, man; read it; and I'll have a word with you after you have done.

Dud. More miracles on foot! So, so, from Lady Rufport.

O'Fla. You're right; it's from her ladyship.

Dud. Well, Sir, I have cast my eye over it; 'tis short and peremptory; are you acquainted with the contents?

O'Fla. Not at all, my dear; not at all.

Dud. Have you any message from Lady Rufport?

O'Fla. Not a syllable, honey; only, when you've digefted the letter, I've a little bit of a message to deliver you from myself.

Dud. And may I beg to know who yourself is?

O'Fla. Dennis O'Flaherty, at your service; a poor major of grenadiers; nothing better.

Dud. So much for your name and title, Sir; now be so good to favour me with your message.

O'Fla. Why then, Captain, I must tell you I have promifed Lady Rufport you shall do whatever it is she bids you to do in that letter there.

Dud. Ay, indeed; have you undertaken so much, Major, without knowing either what she commands, or what I can perform?

O'Fla. That's your concern, my dear, not mine; I must keep my word, you know.

Dud. Or elfe, I suppofe, you and I must meafure swords.

O'Fla. Upon my foul you've hit it.

Dud. That wou'd hardly answer to either of us; you and I have, probably, had enough of fighting in our time before now.

O'Fla. Faith and troth, Master Dudley, you may fay that; 'tis thirty years, come the time, that I have followed the trade, and in a pretty many countries.—Let me fee—In the war before laft I ferv'd in the Irish brigade, d'ye fee; there, after bringing off the French monarch, I left his fervice, with a Britifh bullet in my body, and this ribban in my button-hole. Laft war I followed the fortunes of

the

the German eagle, in the corps of grenadiers; there I had my belly-full of fighting, and a plentiful scarcity of every thing else. After six and twenty engagements, great and small, I went off, with this gash on my scull, and a kiss of the Emprefs Queen's sweet hand, (Heaven bless it!) for my pains. Since the peace, my dear, I took a little turn with the Confederates there in Poland—but such another fet of madcaps!—by the lord Harry, I never knew what it was they were scuffling about.

Dud. Well, Major, I won't add another action to the list; you shall keep your promise with Lady Rusport; she requires me to leave London; I shall go in a few days, and you may take what credit you please from my compliance.

O'Fla. Give me your hand, my dear boy! this will make her my own; when that's the case, we shall be brothers, you know, and we'll share her fortune between us.

Dud. Not so, Major; the man who marries Lady Rusport will have a fair title to her whole fortune without division. But, I hope, your expectations of prevailing are founded upon good reasons.

O'Fla. Upon the best grounds in the world; first, I think she will comply, because she is a woman; secondly, I am persuaded she won't hold out long, because she's a widow; and thirdly, I make sure of her, because I've married five wives, (*en militaire*, Captain) and never failed yet; and, for what I know, they're all alive and merry at this very hour.

Dud. Well, Sir, go on and prosper; if you can inspire Lady Rusport with half your charity, I shall think you deserve all her fortune; at present, I must beg your excuse: good morning to you.   [*Exit.*

O'Fla. A good sensible man, and very much of a soldier; I did not care if I was better acquainted with him: but'tis an awkward kind of country for that; the English, I observe, are close friends, but distant acquaintance. I suspect the old lady has not been over-generous to poor Dudley; I shall give her a little touch about that: upon my soul, I know but one excuse a person can have for giving nothing, and that is, like myself, having nothing to give.   [*Exit.*

S C E N E   IX.

Scene changes to LADY RUSPORT'S *house. A dressing-room.*

MISS RUSPORT *and* LUCY.

Char. Well, Lucy, you've dislodg'd the old lady at last; but methought you was a tedious time about it.

Lucy. A tedious time, indeed; I think they who have le st to spare, contrive to throw the most away; I thought I shou'd never have got her out of the house.

Char. Why, she's as deliberate in canvassing every article of her dress, as an ambassador would be in settling the preliminaries of a treaty.

Lucy. There was a new hood and handkerchief, that had come express from Holborn Hill on the occasion, that took as much time in adjusting——

Char. As they did in making, and she was as vain of them as an old maid of a young lover.

Lucy. Or a young lover of himself. Then, Madam, this being a visit of great ceremony to a person of distinction, at the West end of the town, the old state chariot was dragg'd forth on the occasion, with strict charges to dress out the box with the leopard-skin hammer-cloth.

Char. Yes, and to hang the false tails on the miserable stumps of the old crawling cattle. Well, well, pray Heaven the crazy affair don't break down again with her! at least till she gets to her journey's end.——But where's Charles Dudley? Run down, dear girl, and be ready to let him in; I think he's as long in coming as she was in going.

Lucy. Why, indeed, Madam, you seem the more alert of the two, I must say.   [*Exit.*

Char. Now the deuce take the girl for putting that notion into my head: I'm sadly afraid Dudley does not like me; so much encouragement as I have given him to declare himself, I never could get a word from him on the subject! This may be very honourable, but upon my life it's very provoking. By the way, I wonder how I look to day: Oh! shockingly! hideously pale! like a witch! This is the old lady's glass; and she has left some of her wrinkles on it. How frightfully have I put on my cap! all awry! and my hair dress'd so unbecomingly! altogether, I'm a most complete fright.

SCENE X.

(CHARLES DUDLEY *comes in unobserved.*)

Charles. That I deny.

Char. Ah!

Charles. Quarelling with your glass, cousin? Make it

E   up

up; make it up and be friends; it cannot compliment you
more than by reflecting you as you are.

Char. Well, I vow, my dear Charles, that is delight-
fully said, and deserves my very best curtesy: your flat-
tery, like a rich jewel, has a value not only from its su-
perior lustre, but from its extraordinary scarceness: I
verily think this is the only civil speech you ever directed
to my person in your life.

Charles. And I ought to ask pardon of your good sense
for having done it now.

Char. Nay, now you relapse again: don't you know, if
you keep well with a woman on the great score of beauty,
she'll never quarrel with you on the trifling article of good
sense? But any thing serves to fill up a dull yawning hour
with an insipid cousin; you have brighter moments, and
warmer spirits, for the dear girl of your heart.

Charles. Oh! fie upon you, fie upon you.

Char. You blush, and the reason is apparent; you are a
novice at hypocrisy; but no practice can make a visit of
ceremony pass for a visit of choice: love is ever before its
time; friendship is apt to lag a little after it: pray, Charles,
did you make any extraordinary haste hither?

Charles. By your question, I see you acquit me of the
impertinence of being in love.

Char. But why impertinence? Why the impertinence
of being in love? You have one language for me, Charles,
and another for the woman of your affection.

Charles. You are mistaken; the woman of my affection
shall never hear any other language from me than what I
use to you.

Char. I am afraid then you'll never make yourself un-
derstood by her.

Charles. It is not fit I should; there is no need of love
to make me miserable; 'tis wretchedness enough to be a
beggar.

Char. A beggar, do you call yourself! O Charles,
Charles, rich in every merit and accomplishment, whom
may you not aspire to? And why think you so unworthily
of our sex, as to conclude there is not one to be found
with sense to discern your virtue, and generosity to reward it?

Charles. You distress me; I must beg to hear no more.

Char. Well, I can be silent.——Thus does he always
serve me, whenever I am about to disclose myself to him.

Charles. Why do you not banish me and my misfortunes for ever from your thoughts?

Char. Ay, wherefore do I not, since you never allowed me a place in yours? But go, Sir, I have no right to stay you; go where your heart directs you; go to the happy, the distinguished fair one.

Charles. Now, by all that's good, you do me wrong: there is no such fair one for me to go to, nor have I an acquaintance among the sex, yourself excepted, which answers to that description.

Char. Indeed!

Charles. In very truth: there then let us drop the subject. May you be happy, though I never can!

Char. O Charles! give me your hand; if I have offended you, I ask you pardon: you have been long acquainted with my temper, and know how to bear with its infirmities,

Charles. Thus, my dear Charlotte, let us seal our reconciliation (*kissing her hand.*) Bear with thy infirmities! By Heaven, I know not any one failing in thy whole composition, except that of too great a partiality for an undeserving man.

Char. And you are now taking the very course to augment that failing. A thought strikes me: I have a commission that you must absolutely execute for me; I have immediate occasion for the sum of two hundred pounds; you know my fortune is shut up till I am of age; take this paltry box, (it contains my ear-rings, and some other baubles I have no use for) carry it to our opposite neighbour, Mr. Stockwell, (I don't know where else to apply) leave it as a deposit in his hands, and beg him to accommodate me with the sum.

Charles. Dear Charlotte, what are you about to do? How can you possibly want two hundred pounds?

Char. How can I possibly do without it, you mean? Doesn't every lady want two hundred pounds? Perhaps I have lost it at play; perhaps I mean to win as much to it; perhaps I want it for two hundred different uses.

Charles. Pooh! pooh! all this is nothing; don't I know you never play?

Char. You mistake; I have a spirit to set not only this trifle; but my whole fortune, upon a stake; therefore make no wry faces, but do as I bid you: you will find Mr. Stockwell a very honourable gentleman.

LUCY *enters in haste.*

Lucy. Dear madam, as I live, here comes the old lady in a hackney-coach.

Char. The old chariot has given her a second tumble: away with you; you know your way out without meeting her: take the box, and do as I desire you.

Charles. I must not dispute your orders. Farewell!

[*Exeunt* CHARLES *and* CHARLOTTE.

S C E N E XI.

LADY RUSPORT *enters, leaning on* MAJOR O'FLA-
HERTY's *arm.*

O'Fla. Rest yourself upon my arm; never spare it; 'tis strong enough: it has stood harder service than you can put it to.

Lucy. Mercy upon me, what is the matter; I am frighten'd out of my wits: has your ladyship had an accident?

L. Ruf. O Lucy; the most untoward one in nature: I know not how I shall repair it.

O'Fla. Never go about to repair it, my lady; ev'n build a new one; 'twas but a crazy piece of business at best.

Lucy. Bless me, is the old chariot broke down with you again?

L. Ruf. Broke, child? I don't know what might have been broke, if, by great good fortune, this obliging gentleman had not been at hand to assist me.

Lucy. Dear Madam, let me run and fetch you a cup of the cordial drops.

L. Ruf. Do, Lucy. Alas! Sir, ever since I lost my husband, my poor nerves have been shook to pieces: there hangs his beloved picture; that precious relick, and a plentiful jointure, is all that remains to confole me for the best of men.

O'Fla. Let me see; i'faith a comely perfonage; by his fur cloak I suppose he was in the Russian service; and by the gold chain round his neck, I should guess he had been honoured with the order of St. Catharine.

L. Ruf. No, no; he meddled with no St. Catharines: that's the habit he wore in his mayoralty; Sir Stephen was Lord-Mayor of London: but he is gone, and has left me a poor, weak, solitary widow behind him.

O'Fla.

O'Fla. By all means, then, take a ftrong, able, hearty man to repair his lofs: if fuch a plain fellow as one Dennis O'Flaherty can pleafe you, I think I may venture to fay, without any difparagement to the gentleman in the fur-gown there———

L. Ruf. What are you going to fay? Don't fhock my ears with any compariſons, I defire.

O'Fla. Not I, by my foul; I don't believe there's any comparifon in the cafe.

L. Ruf. Oh, are you come? Give me the drops; I'm all in a flutter.

O'Fla. Hark'e, fweetheart, what are thofe fame drops? Have you any more left in the bottle? I didn't care if I took a little fip of them myfelf.

Lucy. Oh, Sir, they are called the cordial reftorative elixir, or the nervous golden drops; they are only for ladies cafes.

O'Fla. Yes, yes, my dear, there are gentlemen as well as ladies that ftand in need of thofe fame golden drops; they'd fuit my cafe to a tittle.

L. Ruf. Well, Major, did you give old Dudley my let-ter, and will the filly man do as I bid him, and be gone?

O'Fla. You are obey'd; he's on his march.

L. Ruf. That's well; you have manag'd this matter to perfection; I didn't think he would have been fo eafily prevail'd upon.

O'Fla. At the firft word; no difficulty in life; 'twas the very thing he was determined to do, before I came; I never met a more obliging gentleman.

L. Ruf. Well, 'tis no matter; fo I am but rid of him, and his diftreffes: wou'd you believe it, Major O'Flaherty, it was but this morning he fent a begging to me for money to fit him out upon fome wild-goofe expedition to the coaft of Africa, I know not where.

O'Fla. Well, you fent him what he wanted?

L. Ruf. I fent him what he deferved, a flat refufal.

O'Fla. You refufed him!

L. Ruf. Moft undoubtedly.

O'Fla. You fent him nothing!

L. Ruf. Not a fhilling.

O'Fla. Good morning to you—Your fervant—(*going.*)

L. Ruf. Hey-day! What ails the man? Where are you going?

O'Fla,

O'Fla. Out of your houfe, before the roof falls on my head—to poor Dudley, to fhare the little modicum that thirty years hard fervice has left me; I wifh it was more for his fake.

L. Ruf. Very well, Sir; take your courfe; I fhan't attempt to ftop you; I fhall furvive it; it will not break my heart if I never fee you more.

O'Fla. Break your heart! No, o'my confcience will it not.—You preach, and you pray, and you turn up your eyes, and all the while you're as hard-hearted as an hyena— A hyena, truly! By my foul there isn't in the whole creation fo favage an animal as a human creature without pity.   [*Exit.*

L. Ruf. A hyena, truly! Where did the fellow blunder upon that word? Now the deuce take him for ufing it, and the Macaronics for inventing it.

END OF THE SECOND ACT.

ACT III SCENE I.

(*A room in* STOCKWELL'S *houfe.*)

STOCKWELL *and* BELCOUR.

Stock. GRATIFY me fo far, however, Mr. Belcour, as to fee Mifs Rufport; carry her the fum fhe wants, and return the poor girl her box of diamonds, which Dudley left in my hands; you know what to fay on the occafion better than I do; that part of your commiffion I leave to your own difcretion, and you may feafon it with what galantry you think fit.

Bel. You cou'd not have pitch'd upon a greater bungler at galantry than myfelf, if you had rummag'd every company in the city, and the whole court of aldermen into the bargain: part of your errand, however, I will do; but whether it fhall be with an ill grace or a good one, depends upon the caprice of a moment, the humour of the lady, the mode of our meeting, and a thoufand undefinable fmall circumftances that neverthelefs determine us upon all the great occafions of life.

Stock. I perfuade myfelf you will find Mifs Rufport an ingenious, worthy, animated girl.

Bel. Why I like her the better, as a woman; but name her not to me as a wife! No, if ever I marry, it muft be a ftaid, fober, confiderate damfel, with blood in her veins as cold as a turtle's; quick of fcent as a vulture when danger's in the wind; wary and fharp-fighted as a hawk when treachery is on foot: with fuch a companion at my elbow, for ever whifpering in my ear—have a care of this man, he's a cheat; don't go near that woman, fhe's a jilt; over head there's a fcaffold, under foot there's a well: Oh! Sir, fuch a woman might lead me up and down this great city without difficulty or danger; but with a girl of Mifs Rufport's complexion, heaven and earth, Sir! we fhould be dup'd, undone, and diftracted, in a fortnight.

Stock. Ha! ha! ha! Why you are become wond'rous circumfpect of a fudden, pupil; and if you can find fuch a prudent damfel as you defcribe, you have my confent— only beware how you chufe; difcretion is not the reigning quality amongft the fine ladies of the prefent time; and

I think

I think in Miss Rusport's particular I have given you no bad counsel.

Bel. Well, well, if you'll fetch me the jewels, I believe I can undertake to carry them to her; but as for the money, I'll have nothing to do with that; Dudley would be your fittest ambassador on that occasion; and, if I mistake not, the most agreeable to the lady.

Stock. Why, indeed, from what I know of the matter, it may not improbably be destined to find its way into his pockets.   [*Exit.*

Bel. Then, depend upon it, these are not the only trinkets she means to dedicate to Captain Dudley. As for me, Stockwell indeed wants me to marry; but, till I can get this bewitching girl, this incognita, out of my head, I can never think of any other woman.

(SERVANT *enters, and delivers a letter.*)

Heyday! Where can I have picked up a correspondent already! 'Tis a most execrable manuscript—Let me see — Martha Fulmer—Who is Martha Fulmer? Pshaw! I won't be at the trouble of deciphering her damn'd pot-hooks. Hold, hold, hold; what have we got here!

" DEAR SIR,

        " I've discover'd the lady you was so
" much smitten with, and can procure you an interview
" with her; if you can be as generous to a pretty girl as
" you was to a palty old captain," (how did she find that
out!) " you need not despair: come to me immediately;
" the lady is now in my house, and expects you.

                                " Yours,

                                " MARTHA FULMER."

O thou dear, lovely, and enchanting paper, which I was about to tear into a thousand scraps, devoutly I entreat thy pardon: I have slighted thy contents, which are delicious; slander'd thy characters, which are divine; and all the attonement I can make is implicitly to obey thy mandates.

STOCKWELL *returns.*

Stock. Mr. Belcour, here are the jewels; this letter encloses bills for the money; and, if you will deliver it to Miss Rusport, you'll have no farther trouble on that score.

Bel.

Bel. Ah, Sir! the letter which I've been reading difqualifies me for delivering the letter which you have been writing: I have other game on foot; the lovelieft girl my eyes ever feafted upon is ftarted in view, and the world cannot now divert me from purfuing her.

Stock. Hey-day! What has turned yon thus on a fudden?

Bel. A woman: one tnat can turn, and overturn me and my tottering refolutions every way fhe will. Oh, Sir, if this is folly in me, you muft rail at Nature: you muft chide the fun, that was vertical at my birth, and would not wink upon my nakednefs, but fwaddled me in the broadeft, hotteft glare of his meridian beams.

Stock. Mere rhapfody; mere childifh rhapfody; the libertine's familiar plea——Nature made us, 'tis true, but we are the refponfible creators of our own faults and follies.

Bel. Sir!

Stock. Slave of every face you meet, fome huffey has inveigled you, fome handfome profligate, (the town is full of them;) and, when once fairly bankrupt in conftitution, as well as fortune, nature no longer ferves as your excufe for being vicious; neceffity, perhaps, will ftand your friend, and you'll reform.

Bel. You are fevere.

Stock. It fits me to be fo—it well becomes a father——I would fay a friend—How ftrangely I forget myfelf—How difficult it is to counterfeit indifference, and put a mafk upon the heart—I've ftruck him hard; he reddens.

Bel. How could you tempt me fo? Had you not inadvertently dropped the name of father, I fear our friendfhip, fhort as it has been, would fcarce have held me—But even your miftake I reverence—Give me your hand—'tis over.

Stock. Generous young man——let me embrace you—— How fhall I hide my tears? I have been to blame; becaufe I bore you the affection of a father, I rafhly took up the authority of one. I afk your pardon—purfue your courfe; I have no right to ftop it——What would you have me do with thefe things?

Bel. This, if I might advife; carry the money to Mifs Rufport immediately; never let generofity wait for it's materials; that part of the bufinefs preffes. Give me the jewels; I'll find an opportunity of delivering them into her hands; and your vifit may pave the way for my reception. [*Exit.*

Stock. Be it fo: good morning to you. Farewel advice!

F   Away

Away goes he upon the wing for pleafure.   What various
paffions he awakens in me! He pains, yet pleafes me; af-
frights, offends, yet grows upon my heart.   His very fail-
ings fet him off—for ever trefpaffing, for ever atoning, I
aimoft think he would not be fo perfect, were he free from
fault : I muft diffemble longer ; and yet how painful the
experiment !--Even now he's gone upon fome wild adven-
ture ; and who can tell what mifchief may befall him ; O
Nature, what it is to be a father ! Juft fuch a thoughtlefs
headlong thing was I when I beguiled his mother into
love.   [*Exit.*

S C E N E   II.

Scene changes to F U L M E R ' S *Houfe.*

F U L M E R *and his* W I F E.

Ful. I tell you, Patty, you are a fool to think of bringing
him and Mifs Dudley together ; 'twill ruin every thing,
and blow your whole fcheme up to the moon at once.

Mrs. Ful. Why, fure, Mr. Fulmer, I may be allowed
to rear a chicken of my own hatching, as they fay.   Who
firft fprung the thought but I, pray ? Who firft contrived
the plot ? Who propofed the letter, but I, I ?

Ful. And who dogg'd the gentleman home ? Who found
out his name, fortune, connection ; that he was a Weft-
Indian, frefh landed, and full of cafh ; a gull to our heart's
content ; a hot brain'd headlong fpark, that would run
into our trap, like a wheat-ear under a turf ?

Mrs. Ful. Hark ! he's come : difappear, march ; and
leave the field open to my machinations. [*Exit* F U L M E R.

S C E N E   III.

B E L C O U R *enters to her.*

Bel. O, thou dear minifter to my happinefs, let me
embrace thee ! Why thou art my polar ftar, my propitious
conftellation, by which I navigate my impatient bark into
the port of pleafure and delight.

Mrs. Ful. Oh, you men are fly creatures ! Do you remember now, you cruel, what you faid to me this morning ?

Bel. All a-jeft, a frolick ; never think on't ; bury it for
ever in oblivion ; thou ! why thou art all over nectar and
                                                            ambrofia,

ambrofia, powder of pearl and odour of roſes; thou haſt
the youth of Hebe, the beauty of Venus, and the pen of
Sapʒho; but in the name of all that's lovely, where's the
lady? i expected to find her with you.

Mrs. Ful. No doubt you did, and theſe raptures were de-
ſigned for her; but where have you loitered? the lady's
gone, you are too late; girls of her ſort are not to be kept
waiting like negro ſlaves in your ſugar plantations.

Bel Gone! whither is ſhe gone? tell me that I may
follow her.

Mrs. Ful Hold, hold, not ſo faſt young gentleman,
this is a caſe of ſome delicacy; ſhou'd Captain Dudley
know that introduced you to his daughter, he is a man
of ſuch ſcrupulous honour——

Bel. What do you tell me! is ſhe daughter to the old
gentleman i met here this morning?

Mrs Ful. The ſame; him you was ſo generous to.

Bel. There's an end of the matter then at once; it ſhall
never be ſaid of me, that I took advantage of the father's
neceſſities to trepan the daughter *(going).*

Mrs. Ful. So, fo, I've made a wrong caſt, he's one of
your conſcientious ſinners I find; but I won't loſe him
thus——Ha! ha! ha!

Bel What is it you laugh at?

Mrs. Ful Your abſoluce inexperience: have you lived
ſo very little time in this country, as not to know that between young people of equal ages, the term of ſiſter often
is a cover for that of miſtreſs? This young lady is, in that
ſenſe of the word, ſiſter to young Dudley, and conſe-
quently daughter to my old lodger.

Bel. Indeed! are you ſerious?

Mrs Ful. Can you doubt it? I muſt have been pretty
well aſſur'd of that before I invited you hither.

Bel. That's true; ſhe cannot be a woman of honour,
and Dudley is an unconſcionable young rogue to think of
keeping one fine girl in pay, by raiſing contributions on
another; he ſhall therefore give her up; ſhe is a dear, bewitching, miſchievous, little devil; and he ſhall poſitively
give her up.

Mrs. Ful. Ay, now the freak has taken you again; I
ſay give her up; there's one way, indeed, and certain of
ſuccefs.

Bel. What's that?

Mrs. Ful. Out-bid him, never dream of out-bluftring him; buy out his leafe of poffeffion, and leave her to manage his ejectment.

Bel. Is fhe fo venal? Never fear me then; when beauty is the purchafe, I fhan't think much of the price.

Mrs. Ful. All things, then, will be made eafy enough; let me fee; fome little genteel prefent to begin with: what have you got about you? Ay, fearch; I can beftow it to advantage, there's no time to be loft.

Bel. Hang it, confound it; a plague upon't, fay I! I hav'n't a guinea left in my pocket; I parted from my whole ftock here this morning, and have forgot to fupply myfelf fince.

Mrs. Ful. Mighty well; let it pafs then; there's an end; think no more of the lady, that's all.

Bel. Diftraction! think no more of her? let me only ftep home and provide myfelf, I'll be back with you in an inftant.

Mrs. Ful. Pooh, pooh! that's a wretched fhift: have you nothing of value about you? Money's a coarfe flovenly vehicle, fit only to bribe electors in a borough; there are more graceful ways of purchafing a lady's favours; rings, trinkets, jewels!

Bel. Jewels! Gadfo, I proteft I had forgot: I have a cafe of jewels; but they won't do, I muft not part from them; no, no, they are appropriated; they are none of my own.

Mrs. Ful. Let me fee, let me fee! Ay, now, this were fomething-like: pretty creatures, how they fparkle! thefe wou'd enfure fuccefs.

Bel. Indeed!

Mrs. Ful. Thefe wou'd make her your own for ever.

Bel. Then the deuce take 'em for belonging to another perfon; I cou'd find in my heart to give 'em the girl, and fwear I've loft them.

Mrs. Ful. Ay, do, fay they were ftolen out of your pocket.

Bel. No, hang it, that's difhonourable; here, give me the paltry things, I'll write you an order on my merchant for double their value.

Mrs. Ful. An order! No; order for me no orders upon merchants, with their value received, and three days grace; their noting, protefting, and endorfing, and all their counting-houfe formalities; I'll have nothing to do with
them;

them; leave your diamonds with me, and give your order for the value of them to the owner: the money would be as good as the trinkets, I warrant you.

Bel. Hey! how! I never thought of that; but a breach of trust; 'tis impoffible; I never can confent, therefore, give me the jewels back again.

Mrs. Ful. Take 'em; I am now to tell you the lady is in this houfe.

Bel. In this houfe?

Mrs. Ful. Yes, Sir, in this very houfe; but what of that? you have got what you like better; your toys, your trinkets; go, go: Oh! you're a man of a notable fpirit, are you not?

Bel. Provoking creature! Bring me to the fight of the dear girl, and difpofe of me as you think fit.

Mrs. Ful. And of the diamonds too?

Bel. Damn 'em, I wou'd there was not fuch a bauble in nature! But come, come, difpatch; if I had the threne of Dehli I fhould give it to her.

Mrs. Ful. Swear to me then that you will keep within bounds, remember fhe paffes for the fifter of young Dudley. Oh! if you come to your flights, and your rhapfodies, fhe'll be off in an inftant.

Bel. Never fear me.

Mrs. Ful. You muft expect to hear her talk of her father, as fhe calls him, and her brother, and your bounty to her family.

Bel. Ay, ay, never mind what fhe talks of, only bring her.

Mrs. Ful. You'll be prepar'd upon that head?

Bel. I fhall be prepar'd, never fear; away with you.

Mrs. Ful. But hold, I had forgot: not a word of the diamonds; leave that matter to my management.

Bel. Hell and vexation! Get out of the room, or I fhall run diftracted. [*Exit Mrs. Fulmer.*] Of a certain, Belcour, thou art born to be the fool of woman: fure no man fins with fo much repentance, or repents with fo little amendment, as I do. I cannot give away another perfon's property, honour forbids me; and I pofitively cannot give up the girl; love, paffion, conftitution, every thing protefts againft that. How fhall I decide? I cannot bring myfelf to break a truft, and I am not at prefent in the humour to baulk my inclinations. Is there no middle way? Let me confider——

confider—There is, there is: my good genius has prefented me with one; apt, obvious, honourable: the girl fhall not go without her baubles, I'll not go without the girl, Mifs Rufport fhan't lofe her diamonds, I'll fave Dudley from deftruction, and every party fhall be a gainer by the project.

SCENE IV.

MRS. FULMER introducing MISS DUDLEY.

Mrs. Ful. Mifs Dudley, this is the worthy gentleman you wifh to fee; this is Mr. Belcour.

Louifa. As I live, the very man that befet me in the ftreets! *(afide.)*

Bel. An angel, by this light! Oh I am gone paft all retrieving! *(afide.)*

Louifa. Mrs. Fulmer, Sir, informs me you are the gentleman from whom my father has received fuch civilities.

Bel. Oh! never name 'em.

Louifa. Pardon me, Mr. Belcour, they muft be both named and remember'd; and if my father was here——

Bel. I am much better pleafed with his reprefentative.

Louifa. That title is my brother's, Sir; I have no claim to it.

Bel. I believe it.

Louifa. But as neither he nor my father were fortunate enough to be at home, I cou'd not refift the opportunity—

Bel. Nor I neither, by my foul, Madam: let us improve it, therefore. I am in love with you to diftraction; I was charmed at the firft glance; I attempted to accoft you; you fled; I follow'd; but was defeated of an interview; at length I have obtain'd one, and feize the opportunity of cafting my perfon and my fortune at your feet.

Louifa You aftonifh me! Are you in your fenfes, or do you make a jeft of my misfortunes? Do you ground pretences on your generofity, or do you make a practice of this folly with every woman you meet?

Bel. Upon my life, no: as you are the handfomeft woman I ever met, fo you are the firft to whom I ever made the like profeffions: as for my generofity, Madam, I muft refer you on that fcore to this good lady, who I believe has fomething to offer in my behalf.

Louifa.

Louisa. Don't build upon that, Sir; I muſt have better proofs of your generoſity, than the mere diveſtment of a little ſuperfluous drofs, before I can credit the ſincerity of profeſſions ſo abruptly delivered.   *[Exit haſtiy.*

Bel. Oh! ye Gods and Goddeſſes, how her anger animates her beauty!   *[Going out.*

Mrs. Ful. Stay, Sir; if you ſtir a ſtep after her, I renounce your intereſt for ever: why you'll ruin every thing.

Bel. Well, I muſt have her, coſt what it will: I ſee ſhe underſtands her own value tho'; a little ſuperfluous drofs, truly! She muſt have better proofs of my generoſity.

Mrs. Ful. 'Tis exactly as I told you; your money ſhe calls drofs; ſhe's too proud to ſtain her fingers with your coin; bait your hook well with jewels; try that experiment, and ſhe's your own.

Bel. Take 'em; let 'em go; lay 'em at her feet; I muſt get out of the ſcrape as I can; my propenſity is irreſiſtible: there; you have 'em; they are yours; they are her's; but remember they are a truſt; I commit them to her keeping till I can buy 'em off with ſomething ſhe ſhall think more valuable; now tell me when ſhall I meet her?

Mrs. Ful. How can I tell that? Don't you ſee what an alarm you have put her into? Oh! you're a rare one! But go your ways for this while; leave her to my management, and come to me at ſeven this evening; but remember not to bring empty pockets with you——Ha! ha! ha!

        [Exeunt ſeverally.

S C E N E V.

L A D Y R U S P O R T's *Houſe.*

M I S S R U S P O R T *enters, followed by a Servant.*

Char. Deſire Mr. Stockwell to walk in.   *[Exit Servant.*

S T O C K W E L L *enters.*

Stock. Madam, your moſt obedient ſervant: I am honoured with your commands, by Captain Dudley; and have brought the money with me as you directed: I underſtand the ſum you have occaſion for is two hundred pounds.

Char. It is, Sir; I am quite confounded at your taking this trouble upon yourſelf, Mr. Stockwell.

        Stock.

Stock. There is a Bank-note, Madam, to the amount : your jewels are in safe hands, and will be delivered to you directly. If I had been happy in being better known to you, I should have hoped you would not have thought it neceffary to place a depofit in my hands for fo trifling a fum as you have now required me to fupply you with.

Char. The bawbles I fent you may very well be fpared ; and, as they are the only fecurity in my prefent fituation, I can give you, I could wifh you would retain them in your hands : when I am of age, (which, if I live a few months, I fhall be) I will replace your favour, with thanks.

Stock. It is obvious, Mifs Rufport, that your charms will fuffer no impeachment by the abfence of thefe fuperficial ornaments ; but they fhould be feen in the fuite of a woman of fafhion, not as creditors to whom you are indebted for your appearance, but as fubfervient attendants, which help to make up your equipage.

Char. Mr. Stockwell is determined not to wrong the confidence I repofed in his politenefs.

Stock. I have only to requeft, Madam, that you will allow Mr. Belcour, a young gentleman, in whofe happinefs I particularly intereft myfelf, to have the honour of delivering you the box of jewels.

Char. Moft gladly ; any friend of yours cannot fail of being welcome here.

Stock. I flatter myfelf you will not find him totally undeferving your good opinion ; an education, not of the ftricteft kind, and ftrong animal fpirits, are apt fometimes to betray him into youthful irregularities ; but an high principle of honour, and an uncommon benevolence, in the eye of candor, will, I hope, atone for any faults, by which thefe good qualities are not impaired.

Char. I dare fay Mr. Belcour's behaviour wants no apology : we've no right to be over ftrict in canvaffing the morals of a common acquaintance.

Stock. I wifh it may be my happinefs to fee Mr. Belcour in the lift, not of your common, but particular acquaintance, of your friends, Mifs Rufport—I dare not be more explicit.

Char. Nor need you, Mr. Stockwell : I fhall be ftudious to deferve his friendfhip ; and, though I have long fince unalterably placed my affections on another, I truft, I have not left myfelf infenfible to the merits of Mr. Belcour ;

cour ; and hope that neither you nor he will, for that reason, think me lefs worthy your good opinion and regards.

Stock. Mifs Rufport, I fincerely wifh you happy : I have no doubt you have placed your affection on a deferving man ; and I have no right to combat your choice. [*Exit.*

Char. How honourable is that behaviour ! Now, if Charles was here, I fhould be happy. The old lady is fo fond of her new Irifh acquaintance, that I have the whole houfe at my difpofal. [*Exit* CHARLOTTE

SCENE VI.

BELCOUR *enters, preceded by a Servant.*

Ser. I afk your honour's pardon ; I thought my young lady was here : who fhall I inform her wou'd fpeak to her ?

Bel. Belcour is my name, Sir ; and pray beg your lady to put herfelf in no hurry on my account ; for I'd fooner fee the devil than fee her face *(Exit Servant.)* In the name of all that's mifchievous, why did Stockwell drive me hither in fuch hafte ? A pretty figure, truly, I fhall make : an ambaffador without credentials. Blockhead that I was to charge myfelf with her diamonds ; officious, meddling puppy ! Now they are irretrievably gone : that fufpicious jade Fulmer woudn't part even with a fight of them, tho' I would have ranfom'd 'em at twice their value. Now muft I truft to my poor wits to bring me off : a lamentable dependance. Fortune be my helper ! Here comes the girl— If fhe is noble minded, as fhe is faid to be, fhe will forgive me ; if not, 'tis a loft caufe ; for I have not thought of one word in my excufe.

SCENE VII.

CHARLOTTE *enters.*

Char. Mr. Belcour, I'm proud to fee you : your friend, Mr. Stockwell, prepared me to expect this honour ; and I am happy in the opportunity of being known to you.

Bel. A fine girl, by my foul ! Now what a curfed hang-dog do I look like ! *(afide.)*

Char. You are newly arrived in this country, Sir ?

Bel. Juft landed, Madam ; juft fet a-fhore, with a large cargo of Mufcavado fugars, rum-puncheons, mahogany-flabs, wet fweet-meats, and green paroquets.

Char.

Char. May I afk you how you like London, Sir?

Bel. To admiration: I think the town and the town's-folk are exactly fuited; 'tis a great, rich, overgrown, noify, tumultuous place: the whole morning is a buftle to get money, and the whole afternoon is a hurry to fpend it.

Char. Are thefe all the obfervations you have made?

Bel. No, Madam; I have obferved the women are very captivating, and the men very foon caught.

Char. Ay, indeed! Whence do you draw that conclufion?

Bel. From infallible guides; the firft remark I collect from what I now fee, the fecond from what I now feel.

Char. Oh, the deuce take you! But to wave this fubject; I believe, Sir, this was a vifit of bufinefs, not compliment; was it not?

Bel. Ay; now comes on my execution.

Char. You have fome foolifh trinkets of mine, Mr. Belcour; havn't you?

Bel. No, in truth; they are gone in fearch of a trinket, ftill more foolifh than themfelves *(afide.)*

Char. Some diamonds I mean, Sir; Mr. Stockwell inform'd me you was charg'd with 'em.

Bel. Oh, yes, Madam; but I have the moft treacherous memory in life—Here they are! Pray put them up; they're all right; you need not examine 'em *(gives a box.)*

Charl. Hey-dey! right, Sir! Why thefe are not my diamonds; thefe are quite different; and, as it fhould feem, of much greater value.

Bel. Upon my life I'm glad on't; for then I hope you value 'em more than your own.

Char. As a purchafer I fhould, but not as an owner; you miftake; thefe belong to fomebody elfe.

Bel. 'Tis yours, I'm afraid, that belong to fomebody elfe.

Char. What is it you mean? I muft infift upon your taking 'em back again.

Bel. Pray, Madam, don't do that; I fhall infallibly lofe them; I have the worft luck with diamonds of any man living.

Char. That you might well fay, was you to give me thefe in the place of mine; but pray, Sir, what is the reafon of all this? Why have you changed the jewels? and where have you difpofed of mine?

Bel.

Bel. Mifs Rufport, I cannot invent a lie for my life; and, if it was to fave it, I coudn'. tell one : I am an idle diffipated, unthinking fellow, not worth your notice: in fhort, I am a Weft-Indian; and you muft try me according to the charter of my colony, not by a jury of Englifh fpirits: the truth is, I've given away your jewels; caught with a pair of fparkling eyes, whofe luftre blinded theirs, I ferved your property as I fhould my own, and lavifh'd it away, let me not totally defpair of your forgivenefs : I frequently do wrong, but never with impunity ; if your difpleafure is added to my own, my punifhment will be too fevere. When I parted from the jewels, I had not the honour of knowing their owner.

Char. Mr. Belcour, your fincerity charms me; I enter at once into your character, and I make all the allowances for it you can defire. I take your jewels for the prefent, becaufe I know there is no other way of reconciling you to yourfelf; but, if I give way to your fpirit in one point, you muft yield to mine in another : remember I will not keep more than the value of my own jewels: there is no need to be pillaged by more than one woman at a time, Sir.

Bel. Now, may every blefling that can crown your virtues, and reward your beauty, be fhower'd upon you ; may you meet admiration without envy, love without jealoufy, and old age without malady ; may the man of your heart be ever conftant, and you never meet a lefs penitent, or lefs grateful offender, than myfelf !

(*Servant enters and delivers a letter.*)

Char. Does your letter require fuch hafte ?

Ser. I was bade to give it into your own hands, madam

Char. From Charles Dudley, I fee—have I your permiffion ? Good Heaven, what do I read ! Mr. Belcour, you are concern'd in this——" Dear Charlotte, in the " midft of our diftrefs, Providence has caft a benefactor " in our way, after the moft unexpected manner : a " young Weft-Indian, rich, and, with a warmth of " heart peculiar to his climate, has refcued my father from " his troubles, fatisfied his wants, and enabled him to ac- " complifh his exchange : when I relate to you the man- " ner in which this was done, you will be charmed ; I can " only now add, that it was by chance we found out that

" his

" his name is Belcour, and that he is a friend of Mr,
" Stockwell's. I lofe not a moment's time, in making you
" acquainted with this fortunate event, for reafons which
" delicacy obliges me to fupprefs; but, perhaps, if you
" have not received the money on your jewels, you will
" not think it neceffary now to do it, I have the honour
" to be,
                " Dear Madam,
                        " moft faithfully, yours,
                                " CHARES DUDLEY."

Is this your doing, Sir? Never was generofity fo
worthily exerted.

Bel. Or fo greatly overpaid.

Char. After what you have now done for this noble, but
indigent family, let me not fcruple to unfold the whole
fituation of my heart to you. Know then, Sir, (and
don't think the worfe of me for the franknefs of my de-
claration) that fuch is my attachment to the fon of that
worthy officer, whom you relieved, that the moment I
am of age, and in poffeffion of my fortune, I fhou'd hold
myfelf the happieft of women to fhare it with young
Dudley,

Bel. Say you fo, madam! then let me perifh if I don't
love and reverence you above all woman kind; and, if
fuch is your generous refolution, never wait till you're of
age; life is too fhort, pleafure too fugitive; the foul grows
narrower every hour; I ll equip you for your efcape; I'll
convey you to the man of your heart, and away with you
then to the firft hofpitable parfon that will take you in.

Char. O bleffed be the torrid zone for ever, whofe ra-
pid vegetation quickens nature into fuch benignity! Thefe
latitudes are made for politics and philofophy; friendfhip
has no root in this foil. But, had I fpirit to accept your
offer, which is not improbable, woud'nt it be a mortifying
thing, for a fond girl to find herfelf miftaken, and fent
back to her home, like a vagrant; and fuch, for what I
know, might be my cafe.

Bel. Then he ought to be profcribed the fociety of
mankind for ever——Ay, ay, 'tis the fham fifter that
makes him thus indifferent; 'twill be a meritorious office
to take that girl out of the way.

                                        SCENE

S C E N E VIII.

(Servant enters.)

Ser. Mils Dudley to wait on you, madam.

Bel. Who?

Ser. Mils Dudley.

Char. What's the matter, Mr. Belcour? Are you frighted at the name of a pretty girl? 'Tis the filter of him we were fpeaking of—pray admit her.

Bel. The filter! So, fo; he has impofed on her too—this is an extraordinary vifit, truly. Upon my foul, the affurance of fome folks is not to be accounted for.

Char. I infift upon your not running away; you'll be charm'd with Louifa Dudley.

Bel. Oh, yes, I am charmed with her.

Char. You've feen her then, have you?

Bel. Yes, yes, I've feen her.

Char. Well, isn't fhe a delightful girl?

Bel. Very delightful.

Char. Why, you anfwer as if you was in a court of juftice: O' my confcience! I believe you are caught; I've a notion fhe has trick'd you out of your heart.

Bel. I believe fhe has, and you out of your jewels; for, to tell you the truth, fhe's the very perfon I gave 'em to.

Char. You gave her my jewels! Louifa Dudley my jewels? admirable! inimitable! Oh, the fly little jade! but hufh, here fhe comes; I don't know how I fhall keep my countenance. (LOUISA *enters.*) My dear, I'm rejoiced to fee you; how d'ye do? I beg leave to introduce Mr. Belcour, a very worthy friend of mine; I believe, Louifa, you have feen him before.

Lou. I have met the gentleman.

Char. You have met the gentleman: well, Sir, and you have met the lady; in fhort, you have met each other; why then don't you fpeak to each other? How you both ftand! tongue-tied, and fix'd as ftatues——Ha! ha! ha! Why you'll fall afleep by-and-by.

Lou. Fye upon you; fye upon you; is this fair?

Bel. Upon my foul, I never look'd fo like a fool in my life; the affurance of that girl puts me quite down (*afide.*)

Char. Sir—Mr. Belcour—Was it your pleafure to ad-
vance

vance any thing? Not a fyllable. Come, Louifa, women's wit, they fay, is never at a lofs—Nor you neither?
Speechlefs both—Why you was merry enough before this
lady came in.

Lou. I am forry I have been any interruption to your
happinefs, Sir.

Bel. Madam!

Char. Madam! Is that all you can fay? But come, my
dear girl, I won't teaze you : apropos! I muft fhew you
what a prefent this dumb gentleman has made me : are
not thefe handfome diamonds?

Lou. Yes, indeed, they feem very fine; but I am no
judge of thefe things.

Char. Oh, you wicked little hypocrite, you are no
judge of thefe things, Louifa; you have no diamonds,
not you.

Lou. You know I havn't, Mifs Rufport: you know
thofe things are infinitely above my reach.

Char. Ha! ha! ha!

Bel. She does tell a lie with an admirable countenance,
that's true enough.

Lou. What ails you, Charlotte? What impertinence
have I been guilty of that you fhould find it neceffary to
humble me at fuch a rate? if you are happy, long may
you be fo; but, furely, it can be no addition to it to
make me miferable.

Char. So ferious! there muft be fome myftery in this—
Mr. Belcour, will you leave us together? You fee I treat
you with all the familiarity of an old acquaintance already.

Bel. Oh, by all means, pray command me. Mifs
Rufport, I'm your moft obedient! By your condefcenfion
in accepting thefe poor trifles, I am under eternal obli-
gations to you—To you, Mifs Dudley, I fhall not offer
a word on that fubject: you defpife finery; you have a
foul above it; I adore your fpirit; I was rather unpre-
pared for meeting you here; but I fhall hope for an opportunity of making myfelf better known to you. [*Exit.*

S C E N E   IX.

CHARLOTTE *and* LOUISA.

Char. Louifa Dudley, you furprize me; I never faw
you

you act thus before : can't you bear a little innocent rail-
lery before the man of your heart?

Lou. The man of my heart, madam ? Be affured I never
was fo vifionary to afpire to any man whom Mifs Rufport
honours with her choice.

Char. My choice, my dear! Why we are playing at
crofs purpofes : how enter'd it into your head that Mr.
Belcour was the man of my choice ?

Lou. Why, didn't he prefent you with thofe diamonds ?

Char. Well ; perhaps he did—and pray, Louifa, have
you no diamonds ?

Lou. I diamonds truly! Who fhould give me diamonds ?

Char. Who, but this very gentleman: apropos! here
comes your brother———

S C E N E X.

(CHARLES *enters.*)

I infift upon referring our difpute to him : your fifter
and I, Charles, have a quarrel ; Belcour, the hero of your
letter, has juft left us—fome how or other, Louifa's bright
eyes have caught him ; and the poor fellow's fallen defpe-
rately in love with her—(don't interrupt me, huffey)—
Well, that's excufable enough, you'll fay ; but the jet of
the ftory is, that this hair-brain'd fpark, who does nothing
like other people, has given her the very identical jewels,
which you pledged for me to Mr. Stockwell ; and will you
believe that this little demure flut made up a face, and
fqueezed out three or four hypocritical tears, becaufe I
rallied her about it.

Charles. I'm all aftonifhment! Louifa, tell me without
referve, has Mr. Belcour given you any diamonds ?

Lou. None, upon my honour.

Charles. Has he made any profeffions to you ?

Lou. He has ; but altogether in a ftile fo whimfical and
capricious, that the beft which can be faid of them is to
tell you, that they feem'd more the refult of good fpirits
than good manners.

Char. Ay, ay, now the murder's out ; he's in love with
her, and fhe has no very great diflike to him ; truft to my
obfervation, Charles, for that : as to the diamonds, there's
fome miftake about them, and you muft clear it up :
three

three minutes converfation with him will put every thing in a right train; go, go, Charles, 'tis a brother's bufinefs; about it inftantly; ten to one you'll find him over the way at Mr. Stockwell's.

Charles. I confefs I'm impatient to have the cafe clear'd up; I'll take your advice, and find him out: good bye to you.

Char. Your fervant; my life upon it you'll find Belcour a man of honour. Come, Louifa, let us adjourn to my dreffing-room; I've a little private bufinefs to tranfact with you, before the old lady comes up to tea, and interrupts us.

END OF THE THIRD ACT.

ACT IV.   SCENE I.

FULMER's *Houſe.*

FULMER *and* MRS. FULMER.

Ful. PATTY, wasn't Mr. Belcour with you?

Mrs. Ful. He was; and is now ſhut up in my chamber, in high expectation of an interview with Miſs Dudley; ſhe's at preſent with her brother, and 'twas with ſome difficulty I perſuaded my hot-headed ſpark to wait till he has left her.

Ful. Well, child, and what then?

Mrs. Ful. Why then, Mr. Fulmer, I think it will be time for you and me to ſteal a march, and be gone.

Ful. So this is all the fruit of your ingenious project; a ſhameful overthrow, or a ſudden flight.

Mrs. Ful. Why, my project was a mere impromptu, and can at worſt but quicken our departure a few days; you know we had fairly outliv'd our credit here, and a trip to Boulogne is no ways unſeaſonable. Nay, never droop, man—Hark! hark! here's enough to bear charges *ſhewing a purſe.)*

Ful. Let me ſee, let me ſee: this weighs well; this is of the right ſort: why your Weſt-Indian bled freely.

Mrs. Ful. But that's not all: look here! Here are the ſparklers! *(ſhewing the jewels)* Now what d'ye think of my performances? Heh! a fooliſh ſcheme, isn't it—a ſilly woman—?

Ful. Thou art a Judith, a Joan of Arc, and I'll march under thy banners, girl, to the world's end: come, let's begone; I've little to regret; my creditors may ſhare the old books amongſt them; they'll have occaſion for philoſophy to ſupport their loſs; they'll find enough upon my ſhelves: the world is my library; I read mankind— Now, Patty, lead the way.

Mrs. Ful. Adieu, Belcour!   [*Exeunt.*

SCENE II.

CHARLES DUDLEY *and* LOUISA.

Charles. Well, Louiſa, I confeſs the force of what you ſay: I accept Miſs Ruſport's bounty; and, when you ſee

H   my my generous Charlotte, tell her——but have a care, there is a felfifhnefs even in gratitude, when it is too profufe ; to be overthankful for any one favour, is in effect to lay out for another ; the beft return I cou'd make my benefactrefs wou'd be never to fee her more.

Lou. I underftand you.

Charles. We that are poor, Louifa, fhou'd be cautious ; for this reafon, I wou'd guard you againft Belcour ; at leaft till I can unravel the myftery of Mifs Rufport's diamonds ; I was difappointed of finding him at Mr. Stockwell's, and am now going in fearch of him again : he may intend honourably ; but, I confefs to you, I am ftagger'd ; think no more of him, therefore, for the prefent : of this be fure, while I have life, and you have honour, I will protect you, or perifh in your defence.   [*Exit.*

Lou. Think of him no more ! Well, I'll obey ; but if a wand'ring uninvited thought fhould creep by chance into my bofom, muft I not give the harmlefs wretch a fhelter ? Oh ! yes ; the great artificer of the human heart knows every thread he wove into its fabric, nor puts his work to harder ufes than it was made to bear : my wifhes then, my guiltlefs ones, I mean, are free : how faft they fpring within me at that fentence ! Down, down, ye bufy creatures ! Whither wou'd you carry me ? Ah ! there is one amongft you, a forward, new intruder, that, in the likenefs of an offending, generous man, grows into favour with my heart. Fye, fye upon it ! Belcour purfues, infults me ; yet, fuch is the fatality of my condition, that what fhou'd roufe refentment, only calls up love.

S C E N E   III.

(BELCOUR *enters to her.*)

Bel. Alone, by all that's happy !

Lou. Ah !

Bel. Oh ! fhriek not, ftart not, ftir not, lovelieft creature ! but let me kneel, and gaze upon your beauties.

Lou. Sir ! Mr. Belcour, rife ! What is it you do ?

Bel. See, I obey you ; mould me as you will, behold your ready fervant ! New to your country, ignorant of your manners, habits, and defires, I put myfelf into your hands for inftruction ; make me only fuch as you can like yourfelf, and I fhall be happy.

Lou. I muft not hear this, Mr. Belcour ; go ; fhould

he that parted from me but this minute, now return, I tremble for the confequence.

Bel. Fear nothing; let him come: I love you, Madam; he'll find it hard to make me unfay that.

Louifa. You terrify me; your impetuous temper frightens me; you know my fituation; it is not generous to purfue me thus.

Bel. True; I do know your fituation, your real one, Mifs Dudley, and am refolv'd to fnatch you from it; 'twill be a meritorious act; the old Captain fhall rejoice; Mifs Rufport fhall be made happy; and even he, even your beloved brother, with whofe refentment you threaten me, fhall in the end applaud and thank me: Come, thou'rt a dear enchanting girl, and I'm determin'd not to live a minute longer without thee.

Louifa. Hold, are you mad? I fee you are a bold, affuming man, and know not where to ftop.

Bel. Who that beholds fuch beauty can? By Heaven, you put my blood into a flame. Provoking girl! is it within the ftretch of my fortune to content you? What is it you can further afk that I am not ready to grant?

Louifa. Yes, with the fame facility that you beftow'd upon me Mifs Rufport's diamonds. For fhame! for fhame! was that a manly ftory?

Bel. So! fo! thefe devilifh diamonds meet me every where—Let me perifh if I mean't you any harm: Oh! I cou'd tear my tongue out for faying a word about the matter.

Louifa. Go to her then, and contradict it; till that is done, my reputation is at ftake.

Bel. Her reputation! Now fhe has got upon that, fhe'll go on for ever.—What is there I will not do for your fake? I will go to Mifs Rufport.

Louifa. Do fo; reftore her own jewels to her, which I fuppofe you kept back for the purpofe of prefenting others to her of a greater value; but for the future, Mr. Belcour, when you wou'd do a galant action to that lady, don't let it be at my expence.

Bel. I fee where fhe points: fhe is willing enough to give up Mifs Rufport's diamonds, now fhe finds fhe fhall be a gainer by the exchange. Be it fo! 'tis what I wifh'd.—Well, Madam, I will return Mifs Rufport her

own jewels, and you fhall have others of tenfold their
value.

Louifa. No, Sir, you err moſt widely; it is my good
opinion, not my vanity, which you muſt bribe.

Bel. Why, what the devil wou'd fhe have now ?—Mifs
Dudley, it is my wifh to obey and pleafe you, but I have
fome apprehenfion that we miſtake each other.

Louifa. I think we do: tell me, then, in few words,
what it is you aim at.

Bel. In few words, then, and in plain honeſty, I muſt
tell you, fo entirely am I captivated with you, that had
you but been fuch as it would have become me to have call'd
my wife, I had been happy in knowing you by that name;
as it is, you are welcome to partake my fortune, give me
in return your perfon, give me pleafure, give me love;
free, difencumber'd, antimatrimonial love.

Louifa. Stand off, and let me never fee you more.

Bel. Hold, hold, thou dear, tormenting, tantalizing
girl ! Upon my knees I fwear you fhall not ſtir till you've
confented to my blifs.

Louifa. Unhand me, Sir: O Charles ! protect me,
refcue me, redrefs me.   [*Exit.*

S C E N E   IV.

C H A R L E S   D U D L E Y *enters.*

Charles. How's this ! Rife, villain, and defend yourfelf.

Bel. Villain !

Charles. The man who wrongs that lady is a villain—
Draw !

Bel. Never fear me, young gentleman ; brand me for a
coward, if I baulk you.

Charles. Yet hold ! Let me not be too haſty: your
name I think, is Belcour.

Bel. Well, Sir.

Charles. How is it, Mr. Belcour, you have done this
mean, unmanly wrong ; beneath the mafk of generofity to
give this fatal ſtab to our domeſtic peace ? You might have
had my thanks, my bleffing; take my defiance now. 'Tis
Dudley fpeaks to you, the brother, the protector of that
injur'd lady,

Bel. The brother ? Give yourfelf a truer title,

Charles. What is't you mean ?

Be.

Bel. Come, come, I know both her and you : I found you, Sir, (but how or why I know not) in the good graces of Mifs Rufport—(yes, colour at the name !) I gave you no difturbance there, never broke in upon you in that rich and plenteous quarter ; but, when I cou'd have blafted all your projects with a word, fpar'd you, in foolifh pity fpar'd you, nor rouz'd her from the fond credulity in which your artifice had lull'd her.

Charles. No, Sir, nor boafted to her of the fplendid prefent you had made my poor Louifa ; the diamonds, Mr. Belcour ; How was that ? What can you plead to that arraignment ?

Bel. You queftion me too late ; the name of Belcour and of villain never met before : had you enquir'd of me before you utter'd that rafh word, you might have fav'd yourfelf or me a mortal error : now, Sir, I neither give nor take an explanation ; fo, come on ! [*They fight.*

S C E N E V.

Louisa, *and afterwards* O'Flaherty.

Louifa. Hold, hold, for Heaven's fake hold ! Charles ! Mr. Belcour ! Help ! Sir, Sir, make hafte, they'll murder one another.

O'Fla. Hell and confufion ! What's all this uproar for ? Can't you leave off cutting one another's throats, and mind what the poor girl fays to you ? You've done a notable thing, hav'n't you both, to put her into fuch a flurry ? I think, o' my confcience, fhe's the moft frighted of the three.

Charles. Dear Louifa, recollect yourfelf; why did you interfere ? 'Tis in your caufe.

Bel. Now cou'd I kill him for careffing her.

O'Fla. O Sir, your moft obedient ! You are the gentle-man I had the honour of meeting here before ; you was then running off at full fpeed like a Calmuck, now you are tilting and driving like a Bedlamite with this lad here, that feems as mad as yourfelf : 'Tis pity but your country had a little more employment for you both.

Bel. Mr. Dudley, when you've recover'd the lady, you know where I am to be found. [*Exit.*

O'Fla. Well then, can't you ftay where you are, and that will fave the trouble of looking after you ? Yon vo-
latile

latile fellow thinks to give a man the meeting by getting
out of his way : by my foul 'tis a round-about method that
of his. But I think he call'd you Dudley : Hark'e, young
man, are you fon of my friend the old Captain ?

Charles. I am. Help me to convey this lady to her
chamber, and I fhall be more at leifure to anfwer your
queftions.

O'Fla. Ay will I : come along, pretty one ; if you've
had wrong done you, young man, you need look no further for a fecond ; Dennis O'Flaherty's your man for that :
but never draw your fword before a woman, Dudley ;
damn it, never while you live draw your fword before a
woman.   [*Exeunt.*

S C E N E   VI.

L A D Y   R U S P O R T'*s   Houfe.*

L A D Y   R U S P O R T   *and*   S E R V A N T.

Ser. An elderly gentleman, who fays his name is Varland, defires leave to wait on your ladyfhip.

L. Ruf. Shew him in ; the very man I wifh to fee :
Varland, he was Sir Oliver's follicitor, and privy to all
his affairs ; he brings fome good tidings ; fome frefh
mortgage, or another bond come to light ; they ftart up
every day. (V A R L A N D *enters.*) Mr. Varland, I'm glad
to fee you ; you're heartily welcome, honeft Mr. Varland ;
you and I havn't met fince our late irreparable lofs : how
have you paffed your time this age ?

Var. Truly, my lady, ill enough : I thought I muft
have followed good Sir Oliver.

L. Ruf. Alack-a-day, poor man ! Well, Mr. Varland,
you find me here overwhelmed with trouble and fatigue ;
torn to pieces with a multiplicity of affairs ; a great fortune
poured upon me unfought for and unexpected : 'twas my
good father's will and pleafure it fhould be fo, and I muft
fubmit.

Var. Your ladyfhip inherits under a will made in the
year forty-five, immediately after Captain Dudley's marriage with your fifter.

L. Ruf. I do fo, Mr. Varland ; I do fo.

Var. I well remember it ; I engroffed every fyllable ;
but I am furprized to find your ladyfhip fet fo little ftore
by this vaft acceffion.

L. Ruf. Why you know, Mr. Varland, I am a moderate woman; I had enough before; a fmall matter fatisfies me; and Sir Stephen Rufport (Heaven be his portion!) took care I fhoudn't want that.

Var. Very true; very true, he did fo; and I am overjoyed at finding your ladyfhip in this difpofition; for, truth to fay, I was not without apprehenfion the news I have to communicate would have been of fome prejudice to your ladyfhip's tranquility.

L. Ruf. News, Sir! What news have you for me?

Var. Nay, nothing to alarm you; a trifle, in your prefent way of thinking: I have a will of Sir Oliver's you have never feen.

L. Ruf. A will! Impoffible! How came you by it, pray?

Var. I drew it up, at his command, in his laft illnefs: it will fave you a world of trouble: it gives his whole eftate from you to his grandfon, Charles Dudley.

L. Ruf. To Dudley? His eftate to Charles Dudley? I can't fupport it! I fhall faint! You've killed me, you vile man! I never fhall furvive it!

Var. Look'e there now: I proteft, I thought you would have rejoiced at being clear of the incumbrance.

L. Ruf. 'Tis falfe; 'tis all a forgery, concerted between you and Dudley; why elfe did I never hear of it before?

Var. Have patience, my lady, and I'll tell you: By Sir Oliver's direction, I was to deliver this will into no hands but his grandfon Dudley's: the young gentleman happen'd to be then in Scotland; I was difpatch'd thither in fearch of him: the hurry and fatigue of my journey brought on a fever by the way, which confined me in extreme danger for feveral days; upon my recovery, I purfued my journey, found young Dudley had left Scotland in the interim, and am now directed hither; where, as foon I can find him, doubtlefs, I fhall difcharge my confcience, and fulfil my commiffion.

L. Ruf. Dudley then, as yet, knows nothing of this will?

Var. Nothing; that fecret refts with me.

L. Ruf. A thought occurs: by this fellow's talking of his confcience, I fhould guefs it was upon fale *(afide.)* Come, Mr. Varland, if 'tis as you fay, I muft fubmit. I was fomewhat flurried at firft, and forgot myfelf; I afk
your

your pardon : this is no place to talk of bufinefs; ftep with me into my room; we will there compare the will, and refolve accordingly——Oh ! would your fever had you, and I had your paper.   [*Exeunt.*

S C E N E   VII.

Miss Rusport, Charles, *and* O'Flaherty.

Char. So, fo! My lady and her lawyer have retired to clofe confabulation: now, Major, if you are the generous man I take you for, grant me one favour.

O'Fla. Faith will I, and not think much of my generofity neither; for, though it may not be in my power to do the favour you afk, look you, it can never be in my heart to refufe it.

Charles. Cou'd this man's tongue do juftice to his thoughts, how eloquent would he be ! (*afide.*)

Char. Plant yourfelf then in that room: keep guard, for a few moments, upon the enemy's motions, in the chamber beyond; and, if they fhould attempt a fally, ftop their march a moment, till your friend here can make good his retreat down the back-ftairs.

O'Fla. A word to the wife ! I'm an old campaigner; make the beft ufe of your time; and truft me for tying the old cat up to the picket.

Char. Hufh ! hufh ! not fo loud.

Charles. 'Tis the office of a centinel, Major, you have undertaken, rather than that of a field-officer.

O'Fla. 'Tis the office of a friend, my dear boy; and, therefore, no difgrace to a general.   [*Exit.*

S C E N E   VIII.

Charles *and* Charlotte.

Char. Well, Charles, will you commit yourfelf to me for a few minutes ?

Charles. Moft readily; and let me, before one goes by, tender you the only payment I can ever make for your abundant generofity.

Char. Hold, hold ! fo vile a thing as money muft not come between us. What fhall I fay ! O Charles ! O Dudley ! What difficulties have you thrown upon me !

Familiarly

Familiarly as we have lived, I fhrink not at what I'm doing ; and, anxioufly as I have fought this opportunity, my fears almoft perfuade me to abandon it.

Charles. You alarm me !

Char. Your looks and actions have been fo diftant, and at this moment are fo deterring, that, was it not for the hope that delicacy, and not difguft, infpires this conduct in you, I fhould fink with fhame and apprehenfion ; but time preffes ; and I muft fpeak ; and plainly too—Was you now in poffeffion of your grandfather's eftate, as juftly you ought to be ; and, was you inclined to feek a companion for life, fhould you, or fhould you not, in that cafe, honour your unworthy Charlotte with your choice ?

Charles. My unworthy Charlotte ! So judge me Heaven, there is not a circumftance on earth fo valuable as your happinefs, fo dear to me as your perfon ; but to bring poverty, difgrace, reproach from friends, ridicule from all the world, upon a generous benefactrefs ; thievifhly to fteal into an open, unreferved, ingenuous heart, O Charlotte ! dear, unhappy girl, it is not to be done.

Char. Nay, now you rate too highly the poor advantages fortune alone has given me over you : how otherwife could we bring our merits to any ballance ? Come, my dear Charles, I have enough ; make that enough ftill more, by fharing it with me : fole heirefs of my father's fortune, a fhort time will put it in my difpofal ; in the mean while you will be fent to join your regiment ; let us prevent a feparation, by fetting out this very night for that happy country where marriage ftill is free : carry me this moment to Belcour's lodgings.

Charles. Belcour's ?—The name is ominous ; there's murder in it : bloody inexorable honour ! *(afide.)*

Char. D'ye paufe ? Put me into his hands, while you provide the means for our efcape : he is the moft generous, the moft honourable of men.

Charles. Honourable ! moft honourable !

Char. Can you doubt it ? Do you demur ? Have you forgot your letter ? Why, Belcour 'twas that prompted me to this propofal, that promifed to fupply the means, that nobly offer'd his unafk'd affiftance——

(O'FLAHERTY *enters haftily*.)

O'Fla. Run, run, for holy St. Antony's fake, to horfe

I   and

and away! The conference is broke up, and the old lady advances upon a full piedmontefe trot, within piftol-fhot of your encampment.

Char. Here, here, down the back-ftairs! O, Charles, remember me!

Charles. Farewell! Now, now I feel myfelf a coward.

[*Exit.*

Char. What does he mean?

O'Fla. Afk no queftions, but be gone: fhe has cooled the lad's courage, and wonders he feels like a coward. There's a damn'd deal of mifchief brewing between this hyena and her lawyer: egad I'll ftep behind this fcreen and liften: a good foldier muft fometimes fight in ambufh as well as open field (*retires.*)

S C E N E XI.

Lady Rusport *and* Varland.

L. Ruf. Sure I heard fomebody. Hark! No; only the fervants going down the back ftairs. Well, Mr. Varland, I think then we are agreed: you'll take my money; and your confcience no longer ftands in your way.

Var. Your father was my benefactor; his will ought to be facred; but, if I commit it to the flames, how will he be the wifer? Dudley, 'tis true, has done me no harm; but five thoufand pounds will do me much good; fo, in fhort, Madam, I take your offer; I will confer with my clerk, who witneffed the will; and to-morrow morning put it into your hands, upon condition you put five thoufand good pounds into mine.

L. Ruf. 'Tis a bargain: I'll be ready for you: farewell.

[*Exit.*

Var. Let me confider—Five thoufand pounds prompt payment for deftroying this fcrap of paper, not worth five farthings; 'tis a fortune eafily earn'd; yes; and 'tis another man's fortune eafily thrown away: 'tis a good round fum to be paid down at once for a bribe; but 'tis a damn'd rogue's trick in me to take it.

O'Fla. So, fo! this fellow fpeaks truth to himfelf, tho' he lies to other people—but hufh! (*afide*)

Var. 'Tis breaking the truft of my benefactor; that's a foul crime; but he's dead, and can never reproach me with it: and 'tis robbing young Dudley of his lawful pa-

trimony;

trimony; that's a hard cafe; but he's alive, and knows nothing of the matter.

O'Fla. Thefe lawyers are fo ufed to bring off the rogueries of others, that they are never without an excufe for their own (*afide.*)

Var. Were I affured now that Dudley would give me half the money for producing this will, that Lady Rufport does for concealing it, I would deal with him, and be an honeft man at half price; I wifh every gentleman of my profeffion could lay his hand on his heart and fay the fame thing.

O'Fla. A bargain, old gentleman! Nay, never ftart, nor ftare, you wasn't afraid of your own confcience, never be afraid of me.

Var. Of you, Sir; who are you, pray?

O'Fla. I'll tell you who I am; you feem to wifh to be honeft, but want the heart to fet about it; now I am the very man in the world to make you fo; for, if you do not give me up that paper this very inftant, by the foul of me, fellow, I will not leave one whole bone in your fkin that fhan't be broken.

Var. What right have you, pray, to take this paper from me?

O'Fla. What right have you, pray, to keep it from young Dudley? I don't know what it contains, but I am apt to think it will be fafer in my hands than in your's; therefore give it me without more words, and fave yourfelf a beating: do now; you had beft.

Var. Well, Sir, I may as well make a grace of neceffity. There! I have acquitted my confcience, at the expence of five thoufand pounds.

O'Fla: Five thoufand pounds! Mercy upon me! When there are fuch temptations in the law, can we wonder if fome of the corps are a difgrace to it?

Var. Well, you have got the paper; if you are an honeft man, give it to Charles Dudley.

O'Fla. An honeft man! look at me friend, I am a foldier, this is not the livery of a knave; I am an Irifhman, honey; mine is not the country of difhonour. Now, firrah, be gone; if you enter thefe doors, or give Lady Rufport the leaft item of what has paffed, I will cut off both your ears, and rob the pillory of its due.

Var, I wifh I was once fairly out of his fight. [*Exeunt.*

SCENE X.

A Room in STOCKWELL'*s House.*

Stock. I muſt diſcloſe myſelf to Belcour ; this noble in-
ſtance of his generoſity, which old Dudley has been re-
lating, allies me to him at once ; concealment becomes
too painful ; I ſhall be proud to own him for my ſon——
But ſee, he's here.

(BELCOUR *enters, and throws himſelf upon a ſopha.*)

Bel. O my curſt tropical conſtitution ! Wou'd to Heaven I had been dropt upon the ſnows of Lapland, and never
felt the bleſſed influence of the ſun, ſo I had never burnt
with theſe inflammatory paſſions !

Stock. So ſo, you ſeem diſorder'd, Mr. Belcour.

Bel. Diſorder'd, Sir ! Why did I ever quit the ſoil in
which I grew ; what evil planet drew me from that warm
ſunny region, where naked nature walks without diſguiſe,
into this cold contriving artificial country ?

Stock. Come, Sir, you've met a raſcal ; what o'that ?
general concluſions are illiberal.

Bel. No, Sir, I've met reflection by the way ; I've come
from folly, noiſe, and fury, and met a ſilent monitor—
Well, well, a villain ! 'twas not to be pardon'd—pray
never mind me, Sir.

Stock. Alas ! my heart bleeds for him.

Bel. And yet, I might have heard him : now, plague
upon that blundering Iriſhman for coming in as he did ;
the hurry of the deed might palliate the event : deliberate
execution has leſs to plead—Mr. Stockwell, I am bad company to you.

Stock. Oh, Sir ; make no excuſe. I think you have not
found me forward to pry into the ſecrets of your pleaſures
and purſuits ; 'tis not my diſpoſition ; but there are times,
when want of curioſity wou'd be want of friendſhip.

Bel. Ah, Sir, mine is a caſe wherein you and I ſhall
never think alike ; the punctilious rules, by which I am
bound, are not to be found in your ledgers, nor will paſs
current in the compting-houſe of a trader.

Stock. 'Tis very well, Sir ; if you think I can render you
any ſervice, it may be worth your trial to confide in me ;
if not, your ſecret is ſafer in your own boſom.

Bel.

Bel. That fentiment demands my confidence : pray, fit down by me. You muft know, I have an affair of honour on my hands with young Dudley ; and, tho' I put up with no man's infult, yet I wifh to take away no man's life.

Stock. I know the young man, and am appris'd of your generofity to his father ; what can have bred a quarrel between you ?

Bel. A foolifh paffion on my fide, and a haughty provocation on his. There is a girl, Mr. Stockwell, whom I have unfortunately feen, of moft uncommon beauty ; fhe has withall an air of fo much natural modefty, that had I not had good affurance of her being an attainable wanton, I declare I fhou'd as foon have thought of attempting the chaftity of Diana.

S E R V A N T *enters.*

Stock. Hey-dey, do you interrupt us ?

Ser. Sir, there's an Irifh gentleman will take no denial ; he fays he muft fee Mr. Belcour directly, upon bufinefs of the laft confequence.

Bel. Admit him ; 'tis the Irifh officer that parted us, and brings me young Dudley's challenge ; I fhould have made a long ftory of it, and he'll tell you in three words.

O'F L A H E R T Y *enters.*

O'Fla. Save you, my dear ; and you, Sir ! I have a little bit of a word in private for you.

Bel. Pray deliver your commands ; this gentleman is my intimate friend.

O'Fla. Why then, Enfign Dudley will be g'ad to meafure fwords with you, yonder, at the London Tavern, in Bifhopfgate-Street, at nine o'clock---you know the place.

Bel. I do ; and fhall obferve the appointment.

O'Fla. Will you be of the party, Sir? We fhall want a fourth hand.

Stock. Savage as the cuftom is, I clofe with your propofal ; and tho' I am not fully inform'd of the occafion of your quarrel, I fhall rely on Mr. Belcour's honour for the juftice of it ; and willingly ftake my life in his defence.

O'Fla. Sir, you're a gentleman of honour, and I fhall be glad of being better known to you——But hark'e, Belcour, I had like to have forgot part of my errand :

there

there is the money you gave old Dudley; you may tell it
over faith; 'tis a receipt in full; now the lad can put you
to death with a safe confcience, and when he has done
that job for you, let it be a warning how you attempt the
fifter of a man of honour.

Bel. The fifter?

O'Fla. Ay, the fifter; 'tis Englifh, is it not? Or Irifh;
'tis all one; you underftand me, his fifter, or Louifa
Dudley, that's her name I think, call her which you will:
by St. Patrick, 'tis a foolifh piece of a bufinefs, Belcour,
to go about to take away a poor girl's virtue from her,
when there are fo many to be met in this town, who
have difpos'd of their's to your hands.   [*Exit.*

Stock. Why I am thunderftruck! what is it you have
done, and what is the fhocking bufinefs in which I have
engaged? If I underftood him right, 'tis the fifter of
young Dudley you've been attempting: you talk'd to me
of a profeft wanton; the girl he fpeaks of has beauty
enough indeed to inflame your defires, but fhe has honour, innocence and fimplicity to awe the moft licentious
paffion; if you have done that, Mr. Belcour, I renounce
you, I abandon you, I forfwear all fellowfhip or friendfhip with you for ever.

Bel. Have patience for a moment; we do indeed fpeak
of the fame perfon, but fhe is not innocent, fhe is not
young Dudley's fifter.

Stock. Aftonifhing! who told you this?

Bel. The woman where fhe lodges; the perfon who
put me on the purfuit and contriv'd our meetings.

Stock. What woman? What perfon?

Bel. Fulmer her name is: I warrant you I did not
proceed without good grounds.

Stock. Fulmer, Fulmer! Who waits? *(a Servant enters)*
fend Mr. Stukely hither directly; I begin to fee my way
into this dark tranfaction: Mr. Belcour, Mr. Belcour,
your are no match for the cunning and contrivances of
this intriguing town. *(Stukely enters)* pr'ythee, Stukely,
what is the name of the woman and her hufband, who
were ftopt upon fufpicion of felling ftolen diamonds at
our next-door neighbour's, the jeweller?

Stuke. Fulmer.

Stock. So!

Bel. Can you procure me a fight of thofe diamonds?
Stuke.

Stuke. They are now in my hand; I was defir'd to fhow them to Mr. Stockwell.

Stock. Give 'em to me: what do I fee? As I live, the very diamonds Mifs Rufport fent hither, and which I intrufted to you to return.

Bel. Yes, but I betray'd that truft, and gave 'em Mrs. Fulmer to prefent to Mifs Dudley.

Stock. With a view no doubt to bribe her to compliance?

Bel. I own it.

Stock. For fhame, for fhame; and 'twas this woman's intelligence you relied upon for Mifs Dudley's character?

Bel. I thought fhe knew her; by Heaven, I wou'd have died fooner than have infulted a woman of virtue, or a man of honour.

Stock. I think you wou'd, but mark the danger of licentious courfes; you are betray'd, robb'd, abus'd, and, but for this providential difcovery, in a fair way of being fent out of the world with all your follies on your head —Dear Stukely, go to my neighbour, tell him I have an owner for the jewels, and beg him to carry the people under cuftody to the London Tavern, and wait for me there.   [*Exit* Stukely.

I fear the law does not provide a punifhment to reach the villiany of thefe people; but how in the name of wonder cou'd you take any thing on the word of fuch an informer?

Bel. Becaufe I had not liv'd long enough in your country to know how few informers words are to be taken: perfwaded however as I was of Mifs Dudley's guilt, I muft own to you I was ftagger'd with the appearance of fuch innocence, efpecially when I faw her admitted into Mifs Rufport's company.

Stock. Good Heaven! did you meet her at Mifs Rufport's, and cou'd you doubt her being a woman of reputation?

Bel. By you perhaps fuch a miftake cou'd not have been made; but in a perfect ftranger, I hope it is venial: I did not know what artifices young Dudley might have us'd to conceal her character; I did not know what difgrace attended the detection of it.

Stock. I fee it was a trap laid for you, which you have narrowly efcap'd; you addrefs'd a woman of honour with
all

all the loose incense of a profane admirer, and you have drawn upon you the resentment of a man of honour who thinks himself bound to protect her: Well, Sir, you must atone for this mistake. .

Bel. To the lady the most penitent submission I can make is justly due, but in the execution of an act of justice it never shall be said my soul was swayed by the least particle of fear : I have received a challenge from her brother ; now, tho' I wou'd give my fortune, almost my life itself, to purchase her happiness, yet I cannot abate her one scruple of my honour ; I have been branded with the name of villain.

Stock. Ay, Sir, you mistook her character and he mistook yours ; error begets error.

Bel. Villain, Mr. Stockwell, is a harsh word.

Stock. It is a harsh word, and should be unsaid.

Bel. Come, come, it shall be unsaid.

Stock. Or else what follows ? why the sword is drawn, and to heal the wrongs you have done to the reputation of the sister, you make an honourable amends by murdering the brother.

Bel. Murdering !

Stock. 'Tis thus religion writes and speaks the word ; in the vocabulary of modern honour there is no such term—But come, I don't despair of satisfying the one without alarming the other; that done, I have a discovery to unfold that you will then I hope be fitted to receive.

END OF THE FOURTH ACT.

ACT V.   SCENE I.

The London Tavern.

O'FLAHERTY, STOCKWELL, CHARLES, *and* BELCOUR.

O'FLAHERTY.

GEntlemen, well met! you underftand each other's minds, and as I fee you have brought nothing but your fwords, you may fet to without any further ceremony.

Stock. You will not find us backward in any worthy caufe; but before we proceed any further, I would afk this young gentleman, whether he has any explanation to require of Mr. Belcour.

Charles. Of Mr. Belcour none; his actions fpeak for themfelves: but to you, fir, I would fain propofe one queftion.

Stock. Name it.

Charles. How is it, Mr. Stockwell, that I meet a man of your character on this ground?

Stock. I will anfwer you directly, and my anfwer fhall not difpleafe you. I come hither in defence of the reputation of Mifs Dudley, to redrefs the injuries of an innocent young lady.

O'Fla. By my foul the man knows he's to fight, only he miftakes which fide he's to be of.

Stock. You are about to draw your fword to refute a charge againft your fifter's honour ; you would do well, if there were no better means within reach ; but the proofs of her innocence are lodg'd in our bofoms, and if we fall, you deftroy the evidence that moft effectually can clear her fame.

Charles. How's that, Sir?

Stock. This gentleman could beft explain it to you, but you have given him an undeferv'd name that feals his lips againft you: I am not under the fame inhibition, and if your anger can keep cool for a few minutes, I defire I may call in two witneffes, who will folve all difficulties at once. Here, waiter! bring thofe people in that are without.

O'Fla. Out upon it, what need is there for fo much

talking

talking about the matter ; can't you settle your differences firſt, and diſpute about 'em afterwards ?

(FULMER *and Mrs.* FULMER *brought in.*)

Charles. Fulmer and his wife in cuſtody ?

Stock. Yes, Sir, theſe are your honeſt landlord and landlady, now in cuſtody for defrauding this gentleman of certain diamonds intended to have been preſented to your ſiſter. Be ſo good, Mrs. Fulmer, to inform the company why you ſo groſsly ſcandalized the reputation of an innocent lady, by perſuading Mr. Belcour that Miſs Dudley was not the ſiſter, but the miſtreſs, of this gentleman.

Mrs. Ful. Sir, I don't know what right you have to queſtion me, and I ſhall not anſwer till I ſee occaſion.

Stock. Had you been as ſilent heretofore, Madam, it would have ſaved you ſome trouble ; but we don't want your confeſſion. This letter, which you wrote to Mr. Belcour, will explain your deſign ; and theſe diamonds, which of right belong to Miſs Ruſport, will confirm your guilt : the law, Mrs. Fulmer, will make you ſpeak, tho' I can't. Conſtable, take charge of your priſoners.

Ful. Hold a moment : Mr. Stockwell, you are a gentleman that knows the world, and a member of parliament ; we ſhall not attempt to impoſe upon you ; we know we are open to the law, and we know the utmoſt it can do againſt us. Mr. Belcour has been ill uſed to be ſure, and ſo has Miſs Dudley ; and, for my own part, I always condemn'd the plot as a very fooliſh plot, but it was a child of Mrs. Fulmer's brain, and ſhe would not be put out of conceit with it.

Mrs. Ful. You are a very fooliſh man, Mr. Fulmer, ſo prythee hold your tongue.

Ful. Therefore, as I was ſaying, if you ſend her to Bridewell, it won't be amiſs ; and if you give her a little wholeſome diſcipline, ſhe may be the better for that too : but for me, Mr. Stockwell, who am a man of letters, I muſt beſeech you, Sir, not to bring any diſgrace upon my profeſſion.

Stock. 'Tis you, Mr. Fulmer, not I, that diſgrace your profeſſion, therefore begone, nor expect that I will betray the intereſts of mankind ſo far as to ſhew favour to ſuch incendiaries. Take 'em away ; I bluſh

to

to think such wretches should have the power to set two honest men at variance. [*Exeunt* Fulmer, &c.

Charles. Mr. Belcour, we have mistaken each other; let us exchange forgiveness. I am convinced you intended no affront to my sister, and ask your pardon for the expression I was betrayed into.

Bel. 'Tis enough, Sir; the error began on my side, and was Miss Dudley here, I would be the first to atone.

Stock. Let us all adjourn to my house, and conclude the evening like friends: you will find a little entertainment ready for you; and, if I am not mistaken, Miss Dudley and her father will make part of our company. Come, Major, do you consent?

O'Fla. Most readily, Mr. Stockwell; a quarrel well made up, is better than a victory hardly earned. Give me your hand, Belcour; o' my conscience you are too honest for the country you live in. And now, my dear lad, since peace is concluded on all sides, I have a discovery to make to you, which you must find out for yourself, for deuce take me if I rightly comprehend it, only that your aunt Rusport is in a conspiracy against you, and a vile rogue of a lawyer, whose name I forget, at the bottom of it.

Charles. What conspiracy? Dear Major, recollect yourself.

O'Fla. By my soul, I've no faculty at recollecting myself; but I've a paper somewhere about me, that will tell you more of the matter than I can. When I get to the merchant's, I will endeavour to find it.

Charles. Well, it must be in your own way; but I confess you have thoroughly rous'd my curiosity.

[*Exeunt.*

SCENE II.

STOCKWELL's *House.*

Capt. DUDLEY, LOUISA, *and* STUKELY.

Dud. And are those wretches, Fulmer and his wife, in safe custody?

Stuke. They are in good hands, I accompanied them to the Tavern, where your son was to be, and then went

K 2

in fearch of you. You may be fure Mr. Stockwell will enforce the law againft them as far as it will go.

Dud. What mifchief might their curfed machinations have produced, but for this timely difcovery !

Lou. Still I am terrified ; I tremble with apprehenfion left Mr. Belcour's impetuofity and Charles's fpirit fhou'd not wait for an explanation, but drive them both to extremes, before the miftake can be unravell'd.

Stuke. Mr. Stockwell is with them, Madam, and you have nothing to fear ; you cannot fuppofe he wou'd afk you hither for any other purpofe, but to celebrate their reconciliation and to receive Mr. Belcour's attonement.

Dud. No, no, Louifa, Mr. Stockwell's honour and difcretion guard us againft all danger or offence ; he well knows we will endure no imputation on the honour of our family, and he certainly has invited us to receive fatisfaction on that fcore in an amicable way.

Lou. Wou'd to Heaven they were return'd !

Stuke. You may expect them every minute ; and fee Madam, agreeable to your wifh, they are here. [*Exit.*

S C E N E III.

C H A R L E S *enters, and afterwards* S T O C K W E L L *and* O'F L A H E R T Y.

Lou. O Charles, O brother, how cou'd you ferve me fo, how cou'd you tell me you was going to Lady Rufport's and then fet out with a defign of fighting Mr. Belcour ? But where is he ; where is your antagonift ?

Stock. Captain, I am proud to fee you, and you Mifs Dudley, do me particular honour : We have been adjufting, Sir, a very extraordinary and dangerous miftake, which I take for granted my friend Stukely has explain'd to you.

Dud. He has ; I have too good an opinion of Mr. Belcour to believe he cou'd be guilty of a defign'd affront to an innocent girl, and I am much too well acquainted with your character to fuppofe you cou'd abet him in fuch defign ; I have no doubt therefore all things will be fet to rights in very few words when we have the pleafure of feeing Mr. Belcour.

Stock.

Stock. He has only ftept into the compting-houſe and will wait upon you directly : You will not be over ftrict, Madam, in weighing Mr. Belcour's conduct to the minuteft ſcruple ; his manners, paſſions and opinions are not as yet aſſimilated to this climate ; he comes amongſt you a new character, an inhabitant of a new world and both hoſpitality as well as pity recommend him to our indulgence.

SCENE IV.

BELCOUR *enters, bows to* Miſs DUDLEY.

Bel. I am happy and aſham'd to ſee you ; no man in his ſenſes wou'd offend you ; I forfeited mine and err'd againſt the light of the ſun, when I overlook'd your virtues ; but your beauty was predominant and hid them from my fight; I now perceive I was the dupe of a moſt improbable report, and humbly entreat your pardon.

Lou. Think no more it ; 'twas a miſtake.

Bel. My life has been compos'd of little elſe ; 'twas founded in myſtery and has continued in error: I was once given to hope, Mr. Stockwell, that you was to have deliver'd me from theſe difficulties, but either I do not deſerve your confidence, or I was deceiv'd in my expectations.

Stock. When this lady has confirm'd your pardon, I ſhall hold you deſerving of my confidence.

Lou. That was granted the moment it was aſk'd.

Bel. To prove my title to his confidence honour me ſo far with your's as to allow me a few minutes converſation in private with you.   [*She turns to her father.*

Dud. By all means, Louiſa ; come, Mr. Stockwell, let us go into another room.

Charles. And now, major O'Flaherty, I claim your promiſe of a fight of the paper, that is to unravel this conſpiracy of my aunt Ruſport's : I think I have waited with great patience.

O'Fla. I have been endeavouring to call to mind what it was I overheard ; I've got the paper and will give you the beſt account I can of the whole tranſaction.
                                        [*Exeunt.*

SCENE

SCENE V.

BELCOUR *and* LOUISA.

Bel. Mifs Dudley, I have folicited this audience to repeat to you my penitence and confufion: How fhall I atone? What reparation can I make to you and virtue?

Lou. To me there's nothing due, nor any thing demanded of you but your more favourable opinion for the future, if you fhould chance to think of me: Upon the part of virtue I'm not empower'd to fpeak, but if hereafter, as you range thro' life, you fhou'd furprize her in the perfon of fome wretched female, poor as myfelf and not fo well protected, enforce not your advantage, compleat not your licentious triumph, but raife her, refcue her from fhame and forrow, and reconcile her to herfelf again.

Bel. I will, I will; by bearing your idea ever prefent in my thoughts, virtue fhall keep an advocate within me; but tell me, lovelieft, when you pardon the offence, can you, all perfect as you are, approve of the offender? As I now ceafe to view you in that falfe light I lately did, can you, and in the fulnefs of your bounty will you, ceafe alfo to reflect upon the libertine addreffes I have paid you, and look upon me as your reform'd, your rational admirer?

Lou. Are fudden reformations apt to laft; and how can I be fure the firft fair face you meet will not enfnare affections fo unfteady, and that I fhall not lofe you lightly as I gain'd you?

Bel. Becaufe tho' you conquer'd me by furprize, I have no inclination to rebel; becaufe fince the firft moment that I faw you, every inftant has improv'd you in my eyes, becaufe by principle as well as paffion I am unalterably yours, in fhort there are ten thoufand caufes for my love to you, would to Heaven I could plant one in your foft bofom that might move you to return it!

Lou. Nay, Mr. Belcour.——

Bel. I know I am not worthy your regard; I know I'm tainted with a thoufand faults, fick of a thoufand follies, but there's a healing virtue in your eyes that makes recovery certain; I cannot be a villain in your arms.

Lou.

Lou. That you can never be; whomever you shall honour with your choice, my life upon't that woman will be happy; it is not from suspicion that I hesitate, it is from honour; tis the severity of my condition, it is the world that never will interpret fairly in our case.

Bel. Oh, what am I, and who in this wide world concerns himself for such a namelefs, such a friendlefs thing as I am? I see, Mifs Dudley, I've not yet obtain'd your pardon.

Lou. Nay, that you are in full poffeffion of.

Bel. Oh, seal it with your hand then, lovelieft of women, confirm it with your heart; make me honourably happy, and crown your penitent not with your pardon only, but your love.

Lou. My love!——

Bel. By Heav'n my soul is conquer'd with your virtues more than my eyes are ravifh'd with your beauty: Oh, may this soft, this senfitive alarm be happy, be aufpicious! Doubt not, deliberate not, delay not: If happinefs be the end of life, why do we flip a moment?

S C E N E VI.

O'FLAHERTY *enters, and afterwards* DUDLEY *and* CHARLES *with* STOCKWELL.

O'Fla. Joy, joy, joy! sing, dance, leap, laugh for joy! Ha' done making love and fall down on your knees to every saint in the calendar, for they're all on your side and honeft St. Patrick at the head of them.

Charles. O Louifa, such an event! by the luckieft chance in life we have difcover'd a will of my grandfather's made in his laft illnefs, by which he cuts off my Aunt Rufport with a fmall annuity, and leaves me heir to his whole eftate, with a fortune of fifteen thoufand pounds to yourfelf.

Lou. What is it you tell me? O Sir, inftruct me to support this unexpected turn of fortune. [*To her father.*

Dud. Name not fortune; 'tis the work of providence, 'tis the juftice of Heaven that wou'd not suffer innocence to be opprefs'd, nor your bafe aunt to profper in her cruelty and cunning.

[*A fervant whifpers Belcour, and he goes out.*

O'Fla,

O'Fla. You fhall pardon me, Capt. Dudley, but you muft not overlook St. Patrick neither, for by my foul if he had not put it into my head to flip behind the fcreen when your righteous aunt and the lawyer were plotting together, I don't fee how you wou'd ever have come at the paper there, that Mafter Stockwell is reading.

Dud. True my good friend, you are the father of this difcovery, but how did you contrive to get this will from the lawyer?

O'Fla. By force, my dear, the only way of getting any thing from a lawyer's clutches.

Stock. Well, Major, when he brings his action of affault and battery againft you, the leaft Dudley can do is to defend you with the weapons you have put into his hands.

Charles. That I am bound to do, and after the happinefs I fhall have in fheltering a father's age from the viciffitudes of life, my next delight will be in offering you an afylum in the bofom of your country.

O'Fla. And upon my foul, my dear, 'tis high time I was there, for 'tis now thirty long years fince I fat foot in my native country, and by the power of St. Patrick I fwear I think it's worth all the reft of the world put together.

Dud. Ay, Major, much about that time have I been beating the round of fervice, and 'twere well for us both to give over; we have ftood many a tough gale and abundance of hard blows, but Charles fhall lay us up in a little private, but fafe, harbour, where we'll reft from our labours, and peacefully wind up the remainder of our days.

O'Fla. Agreed, and you may take it as a proof of my efteem, young man, that Major O'Flaherty accepts a favour at your hands, for by Heaven I'd fooner ftarve, than fay I thank you to the man I defpife: But I believe you are an honeft lad, and I'm glad you've trounc'd the old cat, for on my confcience I believe I muft otherwife have married her myfelf to have let you in for a fhare of her fortune.

Stock. Hey day, what's become of Belcour?

Lou. One of your fervants call'd him out juft now and feemingly on fome earneft occafion.

Stock.

Stock. I hope, Miſs Dudley, he has aton'd to you as a gentleman ought.

Lou. Mr. Belcour, Sir, will always do what a gentleman ought, and in my caſe I fear only you will think he has done too much.

Stock. What has he done; and what can be too much? Pray Heaven, it may be as I wiſh !   *[aſide.*

Dud. Let us hear it, child.

Lou. With confuſion for my own unworthineſs, I confeſs to you he has offer'd me ——

Stock. Himſelf.

Lou. 'Tis true.

Stock. Then I am happy; all my doubts, my cares are over, and I may own him for my ſon.——Why theſe are joyful tidings : come, my good friend, aſſiſt me in diſpoſing your lovely daughter to accept this returning prodigal; he is no unprincipled, no harden'd libertine; his love for you and virtue is the ſame.

Dud. 'Twere vile ingratitude in me to doubt his merit—What ſays my child ?

O'Fla. Begging your pardon now, 'tis a frivolous ſort of a queſtion, that of yours; for you may ſee plainly enough by the young lady's looks, that ſhe ſays a great deal, though ſhe ſpeaks never a word.

Charles. Well, ſiſter, I believe the Major has fairly interpreted the ſtate of your heart.

Lou. I own it; and what muſt that heart be, which love, honour and beneficence like Mr. Belcour's can make no impreſſion on ?

Stock. I thank you: What happineſs has this hour brought to paſs !

O'Fla. Why don't we all ſit down to ſupper then and make a night on't.

Stock. Hold, here comes Belcour.

S C E N E VII.

BELCOUR *introducing* Miſs RUSPORT.

Bel. Mr. Dudley, here is a fair refugee, who properly comes under your protection; ſhe is equipt for Scotland, but your good fortune, which I have related to her, ſeems inclin'd to ſave you both the journey——

Nay,

Nay, Madam, never go back; you are amongſt friends.

Charles. Charlotte!

Char. The ſame; that fond officious girl, that haunts you every where; that perſecuting ſpirit——

Charles. Say rather, that protecting angel; ſuch you have been to me.

Char. O Charles, you have an honeſt, but proud heart.

Charles. Nay, chide me not, dear Charlotte.

Bel. Seal up her lips then; ſhe is an adorable girl; her arms are open to you; and love and happineſs are ready to receive you.

Charles. Thus then I claim my dear, my deſtin'd wife.

[*embracing her.*

S C E N E   VIII.

Lady R U S P O R T *enters.*

Lady Ruſ. Heyday! mighty fine! wife truly! mighty well! kiſſing, embracing—did ever any thing equal this? Why you ſhamelefs huſſey!—But I won't condeſcend to waſte a word upon you.——You, Sir, you, Mr. Stockwell, you fine, ſanctified, fair-dealing man of conſcience, is this the principle you trade upon? Is this your neighbourly ſyſtem, to keep a houſe of reception for run-away daughters, and young beggarly fortune-hunters?

O'Fla. Be advis'd now, and don't put yourſelf in ſuch a paſſion; we were all very happy till you came.

Lady Ruſ. Stand away, Sir; hav'nt I a reaſon to be in a paſſion?

O'Fla. Indeed, honey, and you have, if you knew all.

Lady Ruſ. Come, Madam, I have found out your haunts; diſpoſe yourſelf to return home with me: young man, let me never ſee you within my doors again: Mr. Stockwell, I ſhall report your behaviour, depend on it.

Stock. Hold, Madam, I cannot conſent to loſe Miſs Ruſport's company this evening, and I am perſuaded you won't inſiſt upon it; 'tis an unmotherly action to interrupt your daughter's happineſs in this manner, believe me it is.

Lady Ruſ.

Lady Ruf. Her happiness truly ; upon my word ! and I suppose it's an unmotherly action to interrupt her ruin ; for what but ruin must it be to marry a beggar ? I think my sister had a proof of that, Sir, when she made choice of you.   [*To Captain* Dudley.

Dud. Don't be too lavish of your spirits, Lady Rusport.

O'Fla. By my soul you'll have occasion for a sip of the cordial Elixir by and bye.

Stock. It don't appear to me, Madam, that Mr. Dudley can be call'd a beggar.

Lady Ruf. But it appears to me, Mr. Stockwell ; I am apt to think a pair of colours cannot furnish settlement quite sufficient for the heiress of Sir Stephen Rusport.

Char. But a good estate in aid of a commission may do something.

Lady Ruf. A good estate, truly ! where shou'd he get a good estate pray ?

Stock. Why suppose now a worthy old gentleman on his death-bed should have taken it in mind to leave him one——

Lady Ruf. Hah ! what's that you say ?

O'Fla. O ho! you begin to smell a plot, do you ?

Stock. Suppose there should be a paper in the world that runs thus —— " I do hereby give and bequeath all " my estates, real and personal, to Charles Dudley, son " of my late daughter Louisa, &c. &c. &c."

Lady Ruf. Why I am thunder-struck ! by what contrivance, what villany did you get possession of that paper?

Stock. There was no villany, Madam, in getting possession of it ; the crime was in concealing it, none in bringing it to light.

Lady Ruf. Oh, that cursed lawyer, Varland !

O'Fla. You may say that, faith, he is a cursed lawyer, and a cursed piece of work I had to get the paper from him ; your ladyship now was to have paid him five thousand pounds for it, I forc'd him to give it me of his own accord for nothing at all, at all.

Lady Ruf. Is it you that have done this ? Am I foil'd by your blundering contrivances, after all ?

O'Fla. 'Twas a blunder, faith, but as natural a one as if I'd made it o' purpose.

L 2

Charles.

Charles. Come, let us not opprefs the fallen; do right even now, and you fhall have no caufe to complain.

Lady Ruf. Am I become an object of your pity then? Infufferable! confufion light amongft you! marry and be wretched: let me never fee you more.   [*Exit.*

Char. She is outrageous; I fuffer for her, and blufh to fee her thus expofed.

Charles. Come, Charlotte, don't let this angry woman difturb our happinefs: we will fave her in fpite of her-felf; your father's memory fhall not be ftained by the difcredit of his fecond choice.

Char. I truft implicitly to your difcretion, and am in all things yours.

Bel. Now, lovely but obdurate, does not this ex-ample foften?

Lou. What can you afk for more? Accept my hand, accept my willing heart.

Bel. O blifs inutterable! brother, father, friend, and you the author of this general joy——

O'Fla Bleffing of St. Patrick upon us all! 'tis a night of wonderful and furprizing ups and downs: I wifh we were all fairly fet down to fupper, and there was an end on't.

Stock. Hold for a moment! I have yet one word to interpofe—Intitled by my friendfhip to a voice in your difpofal, I have approv'd your match; there yet remains a father's confent to be obtain'd.

Bel. Have I a father?

Stock. You have a father: did not I tell you I had a difcovery to make? Compofe yourfelf: you have a father, who obferves, who knows, who loves you.

Bel. Keep me no longer in fufpence; my heart is foften'd for the affecting difcovery, and nature fits me to receive his blefing.

Stock. I am your father.

Bel. My father? Do I live?

Stock. I am your father.

Bel. It is too much; my happinefs o'erpowers me; to gain a friend and find a father is too much; I blufh to think how little I deferve you.   [*They embrace.*

Dud. See, children, how many new relations fpring from this night's unforefeen events, to endear us to each other.

O'Fla.

O'Fla. O my confcience, I think we fhall be all related by and bye.

Stock. How happily has this evening concluded, and yet how threatning was its approach ! let us repair to the fupper room, where I will unfold to you every circumftance of my myfterious ftory. Yes, Belcour, I have watch'd you with a patient, but enquiring eye, and I have difcover'd thro' the veil of fome irregularities, a heart beaming with benevolence, an animated nature, fallible indeed, but not incorrigible ; and your election of this excellent young lady makes me glory in acknowledging you to be my fon.

Bel. I thank you, and in my turn glory in the father I have gained : fenfibly impreft with gratitude for fuch extraordinary difpenfations, I befeech you, amiable Louifa, for the time to come, whenever you perceive me deviating into error or offence, bring only to my mind the Providence of this night, and I will turn to reafon and obey.

END OF THE PLAY.

EPILOGUE.

Written by D. G. Esq.

SPOKEN BY

Mrs. ABINGTON.

N. B. The Lines in Italics are to be spoken in a catechise Tone.

CONFESS, good folks, has not Miss Rusport shewn,
   Strange whims for SEVENTEEN HUNDRED SEVENTY-ONE?
What, pawn her jewels!——there's a precious plan!
To extricate from want a brave *old* man;
And fall in love with poverty and honour;
A girl of fortune, fashion!——Fie upon her.
But do not think we females of the stage,
So dead to the refinements of the age,
That we agree with our old fashion'd poet:
I am point blank against him, and I'll shew it:
And that my tongue may more politely run,
Make me a lady——Lady Blabington.
Now, with a rank and title to be free,
I'll make a catechism—and you shall see,
What is the *veritable Beaume de Vie* :
As I change place, I stand for that, or this,
My Lady questions first——then answers Miss.

(She speaks as my Lady.)

" Come, tell me, Child, what were our modes and dress,
" In those strange times of that old fright Queen Bess ?"——
And now for Miss——

(She changes place, and speaks for Miss.)

     When Bess was England's queen,
Ladies were dismal beings, seldom seen ;
They rose betimes, and breakfasted as soon
On beef and beer, then studied Greek till noon ;
Unpainted cheeks with blush of health did glow,
Beruff'd and fardingal'd from top to toe,
Nor necks, nor ancles would they ever shew.

Learnt Greek!—*(laughs.)*—Our outside head takes half a day;
Have we much time to dress the *inside,* pray?
No heads dress'd *à la Greque*; the ancients quote,
There may be learning in a *papillote* :

EPILOGUE.

Cards are *our* claſſicks; and I, Lady B,
In learning will not yield to any ſhe,
Of the late founded *female* univerſity.
But now for Lady Blab————

(Speaks as my Lady.)

" Tell me, Miſs Nancy,
" What ſports and what employments did they fancy ?"

(Speaks as Miſs.)

The vulgar creatures ſeldom left their houſes,
But taught their children, work'd, and lov'd their ſpouſes;
The uſe of cards at Chriſtmas only knew,
They play'd for little, and their games were few,
One-and-thirty, Put, All-fours, and Lantera Loo ;
They bore a race of mortals ſtout and boney,
And never heard the name of Macaroni.————

(Speaks as my Lady.)

" Oh brava, brava! that's my pretty dear————
" Now let a modern, modiſh fair appear;
" No more of theſe old dowdy maids and wives,
" Tell how ſuperior beings paſs their lives."————

(Speaks as Miſs.)

Till noon they ſleep, from noon till night they dreſs,
From night till morn they game it more or leſs,
Next night the ſame ſweet courſe of joy run o'er,
Then the night after as the night before,
And the night after that, encore, encore !————

(She comes forward.)

Thus with our cards we *ſhuffle* off all ſorrow,
To morrow, and to-morrow, and to-morrow !
We *deal apace*, from youth unto our prime,
To the laſt moment of our *tabby*-time ;
And all our yeſterdays, from rout and drum,
Have lighted fools with empty pockets home.
Thus do our lives with rapture roll away,
Not with the nonſenſe of our author's play ;
This is true life—true ſpirit—give it praiſe ;
Don't ſnarl and ſigh for good Queen Beſs's days :
For all you look ſo ſour, and bend the brow,
You all rejoice with me, you're living now.